Beyond Everyday Secrets

Ernest Langston

ISBN-10: 1497422892
ISBN-13: 978-1497422896

DEDICATION

This book is dedicated to the fearless, the young at heart, and individuals who never surrender their dreams.

CONTENTS

ACKNOWLEDGMENTS

I acknowledge Buck, my four-legged friends who were with me when I wrote this story, and the readers who support indie published books.

PROLOGUE

What I am about to tell you will forever change your perspective on secrecy, friendship, and consequence. My name is Jack Marshall and, in many ways, I am no different than you. I'm not rich, famous, or gifted in any extraordinary way. Each day after work, after my commute, I find myself parking my average car on my average street like everyone else, and I wouldn't have it any other way. And by the end of this story, I hope that you'll have a greater understanding for this sentiment.

Shortly after this life event happened to me, which will soon be explained, I purchased a train ticket to take me 3000 miles away from California, making a single transfer in Chicago. For the next four days, I slept in seats next to several different strangers until arriving at my destination. During this journey, I held countless conversations with forgettable people, except for one person. On my last night, drinking alone in the dining car, an attractive, middle-aged woman approached me and sat down.

"Didn't anyone tell you that drinking alone leads to trouble?," she questioned. "Let's drink together, what do you say?"

After accepting her first drink, she took it upon herself to pick up the tab for the remaining part of the evening. Who was I to disagree? We soon moved our conversation from the bar to a corner booth and continued without missing a beat. I must be honest with you, I figured she was a lonely, married woman who wanted to lead me back to her cabin. However, within the hour, I discovered my assumptions were wrong, but not completely.

"There is something about your eyes. I don't know… something familiar. I can't put my finger on it, but they're as if they don't belong to you, like you've seen more than you should have for a person your age," she said, gently laying her hand upon mine. "Would you mind if I told you something?"

"Please, do. Be my guest."

"That's real nice of you, but if at any time you wish me to stop, you must let me know, okay?"

"Sure. Now, what would you like to tell me?"

I didn't know what I had agreed to or why she felt secure enough to confide in me. I merely listened and kept drinking. She began by asking my age and made several comments on youth and how wonderful it must feel to live a life so free, to come and go as one wishes, a courageous life brimming with so much freedom that anything surrenders itself as possible. She continued romancing on the thought of a carefree life before pausing and lowering her eyes to her age-spotted hands. And in that moment, I witnessed her vivacious manner quickly shrink, runaway and hide into a dark corner within her mind.

"Is everything okay?," I asked.

"Yes, yes, of course. Sorry. Sometimes, my thoughts become jumbled and crash into each other. High-pitch ringing in my ears, sometimes. I can't stand it. I've learned to stop for a moment and clear the mess, clear my mind. Reset myself, get things back on track again, you know…."

I smiled and waved it off as if it was nothing, blaming it on the cheap alcohol, the late hour, the fatigue of travel, anything, but the truth. I, too, have no control over that high-pitch ringing in my ears, and I can't escape the horrifying images that I've helped create. They've been burned into my memory, forever haunting me as they please, having their way with me whenever they choose. These consequences are no less escapable than my own shadow. And like her, I must learn to live with them. There is no other choice.

She said, "I didn't start off this way, not with having jumbled thoughts and all the rest, and not being able to forget when and where it all started. I can still see it as if it happened yesterday, but it didn't. It happened when I was 15 years old, but that's a problem all its own; one problem at a time, right?"

She spoke of her days as a teenager in the South and of its taboos and of her parents, and how her father had to travel for work, always bringing her "a gift from the road," as he would put it, and of her mother's idiosyncrasies for keeping an organized house. She eventually told me her secret.

"It wasn't planned, the sex, I mean, we just... I don't know. We were young and acting as so, kissing and all, and one thing led to another and— I said, no. I'd never been with a boy before, and— well, that was a very long time ago," she said, taking a drink from her glass. "Things were far more different then, very small town thinking. Turn a blind eye. No one knows nothing; that sort of thing. You understand. Yes, it's true; I should've known better, but I was young and in love. Well, so I thought. I mean, what does any teenage girl really know about true love?"

A gleam intermittently appeared and disappeared in her green eyes as she continued confiding in me. She explained her parents' fury after learning of her pregnancy, but quickly admitted that it was the disappointment that she had caused them that resonated louder than all of the crying, yelling, and screaming combined.

"It's strange how the mind works, don't you think? I mean, if you asked me what I ate for breakfast yesterday, I couldn't tell you without some sort of uncertainty, but I remember my mother's words down to each syllable. That's something that I'll never forget, not that I haven't tried, because I have. I still try, but those things stay with a person and probably always will. I'm certain they will. At times, I can still smell my father's cigarette burning away in that red ashtray… well, it looks like we could use another drink or two," she said with a forced smile and turned away toward the bartender.

After the abortion and being sent North to live with her aunt's family, she found solace in her studies and eventually earned acceptance to a nursing program, leading her farther North.

"I had never been so happy, but I had to work at allowing myself the enjoyment of this blessing. I was forgiven and trusted with life again," she said with tenderness. "I made new friends and my teachers liked me, but what was most important to me at that time was how I was distancing myself from my past, so I thought. I would love to believe that we could escape from our past. I really would love to believe that, but I know better. I know the truth, and no one can escape the truth…."

As we continued drinking, she ventured on, explaining her years as a nurse, and although she found the hours difficult at times, she also found great satisfaction in this type of work. She reminisced on how wonderful it felt knowing that she had helped complete strangers in need.

"I was given a purpose. I was placed there for a specific reason, you know, to help people; and let me tell you, there's nothing better than knowing that, that you are doing good in this… this fucked up world. Sorry, if that offends you, but it's true. Things happen to people like us. We're nothing special. It doesn't mean we're bad people; it just means we're average, and that's fine. Most people are average, good-hearted, hard-working people; they love their country and all that stuff. I mean, here we are, just two people riding the same train, talking and traveling in the same direction. That's it. Nothing more, nothing less, right? It seems pretty simple. Now, what if I told you that we were supposed to meet, you and I? We don't know each other. Did you know that we would be talking over drinks when I walked in? Well, neither did I. But here we are. There's a reason for it. And, that's what I'm taking about. I can't explain this anymore than that, so don't ask," she said with slurred speech. "That's right. I can't tell you the reason anymore than I could tell you why I couldn't save that baby's life. We make choices, we have to, some good and some— well, we learn to live with those ones. It was really nice talking to you, but I need to go to bed now. It's very late for me."

She thanked and wished me a good life and goodnight, then disappeared from my presence as quickly as she arrived, never to been seen again. I felt sad for her and, to be completely honest about it, I also felt connected to her in some unexplainable way other than what will soon be revealed to you. As she confided in me, I am confiding in you, because chances are that we will never meet, nor you will remember my name.

We are two perfect strangers, you and I. Both milling about our private lives, going about our taut routines, saying and doing what we must to get through each day, wanting to believe that our efforts truly carry influence over our destiny. Sooner or later, if you are so lucky, you will discover that we have as much control over own our lives, as we do over the stars in the sky. By the end of this book, I hope you will be one step closer to this discovery. And one day, you will be able to select a perfect stranger without thought and lighten your burden and, possibly, within those brief moments of connection, you may leave an indelible impression in your wake, as that unforgettable woman has done to me.   My story occurred in 1992, over the course of two days.

CHAPTER 1

The temperature had dropped, and the sun now turned the sky into a heavenly pastel mixture of reds, blues, yellows, and purples, varying shades, reminding me of an uncertain memory that I possibly once had of a watercolor painting resting on someone's wall. The motionless clouds, all streaked with muted pinks and grays and all perfectly placed, created some unexplained bittersweet feeling within me. I searched for an explanation, some sort of logical reason for these opposing emotions, but found none, so I pulled the last drag from my joint and exhaled the cloud of smoke toward the horizon, watching it disappear before my eyes.

On the middle school's roof, located six blocks from my house, is where I'd go to be alone and smoke a joint in peace. It became my unofficial Friday night ritual. Typically, I'd meet one of my clients on the bench closest to the multiuser water fountain around dusk, giving myself enough time to do the exchange, pocket the cash, and offer a few words of warning, then watch them slowly fade away into the distance. They were happy and I was at least one or two hundred bucks richer.

It appeared that this once part-time, summer job had seamlessly become my full-time occupation. I tried closing my operation twice, figuring it was the best thing to do for myself, but the truth is, my clients had habitual tendencies. They took comfort in knowing I was reliable, dependable, and I had no interest in wasting my time with just anyone who had a few bucks in their pockets and a desire to get high. I was selective. The exchange was always short, sweet, and simple.

In other words, I either knew you or I didn't, and my clients welcomed and appreciated this quality. I called them clients, not because I was trying to portray myself as some sort of big shot, big time motherfucker, because I wasn't; it's because I knew what they were; and although, they were good, everyday people, they were not my friends, in the true sense of the word. They were what they were. My clients. You understand, right? My true friends were, and still are, Ray, Crumbs, and Charlie. Well, all but one, but I'll get to that later. Now, these guys, these fucking guys were my best friends to the end. They were the brothers that I never had. Now, if you ever had friends like mine, then you completely understand how deep friendships can run and won't question the things we did for each other.

However, on the other hand, if you never experienced undeniable friendship, well, then, chances are that you never will, because this type of true friendship takes years to build and maintain. Now, I'm not talking some typical, college, fraternity brotherhood crap where they make you pledge and force you to wear a heavy backpack or lame sweater with Greek letters on it or some two-day, weekend bonding bullshit that happens in Las Vegas or in the woods or wherever. The friendship I'm talking about is real, as real as it could ever get. By real, I mean, the kind of real shit that you wish never happened; the same kind of shit that you know had to happen. That's what I'm talking about, and if it's all too confusing right now, it's totally understandable, but when you finish this book, you will realize that the same could happen to you; perhaps, not the same situation, detail by detail, but in the same position, you're fucked if you do and you're fucked if you don't, so fuck it. They say you feel most alive before all hell breaks loose. And, you want to know what? They're fucking right.

Each weekend would begin at Ray's house.

It was actually his parent's house, but that was nothing more than a technicality. Ray's mom, a large, soft-spoken woman with a kind smile, was the type of person who always greeted me with a hug. Even when I thought of myself as too cool for one, she'd reel me in and say, "There's gonna come a day when I won't be able to give you boys hugs anymore, so I gotta do it while I can. Now, come here and let me hug you. You're gonna miss these one day, Jack. Trust me," and she wasn't lying.

This weekend, Ray's parents decided to take the RV up North toward Mendocino County to do some camping and fishing, that sort of thing, leaving Ray to his own devices. Now, upon meeting Ray, you would think that he wasn't fond of shaving, haircuts, physical exercise, or making sure that his fly was zipped up, and you'd be right. But what he lacked in grooming and appearance, he made up for in unwavering friendship. I mean, sure, Ray had shaggy hair, was too lazy to shave on most days, didn't see the point of exercise, or cared if his fly was up or down. In his mind, he had transcended all those physical, superficial things. He was the kind of guy that, if you came knocking at his bedroom window at three in the morning on any given day, he would open one eye, look you straight in the face and say, "Well, just don't stand there. Come inside," then close his eye and fall back asleep. I know this to be true, because in my youth, I tried it one September morning, scared shitless, minutes after some Mexican gangster shoved his handgun in my face and threatened my life.

Luckily, the gangster realized that I wasn't the guy he was looking for and decided to let me go. He could've easily pulled the trigger, but he didn't. Instead, he kicked this one guy in the head, which produced a sound something like kicking a sandbag and snapping a celery stick. Later, after the gangster left the apartment, I discovered that he had kicked that guy so hard on the side of his head that it split that guy's ear in two parts, top and bottom. Blood flowed over the white, lacerated cartilage that once connected the ear's outer rim. He took all the cash and cocaine on hand and warned me to find another connection, because the next time he decided to drop by unexpectedly, no one would be walking out of the apartment.

I still remember his name, but there isn't any need to mention it. I mean, what's the point? If you were so fortunate to be released from a trapper's snare, would you look back? The truth behind me being there, in that unfamiliar apartment, that evening was simple. When asked by a casual friend, if I'd like to go to the record store with him, I agreed. Why not? It was nothing more than that, to the record store and back, and I was bored. I love music, and in those days, music wasn't sold over the computer. Most people didn't even own a home computer, and if they did, they didn't really know how to use it. Back then, computers looked like old televisions sitting on top of beige suitcases. I'm not even going to mention the Internet. Shit, man, people were still walking around with Walkmans and cassette tapes in their pockets; and if you had a portable CD player, well, you probably also had your hair frosted. He said that he had to make a quick stop at his buddy's place, and it shouldn't take more than a minute, had to drop off some money or something like that, and that I should come in and smoke a joint. It sounded fine to me. However, by the time, we finished smoking a joint, that's when it all went bad, but it could've gotten worse, way worse. You understand. Anyway, I apologize for my digression, but I now realize that all of these past incidents, good and bad, are tied together, even up to this exact moment in time. Yes, even you choosing to read this book, is yet another cobblestone on your personal path. If asked why you chose this particular book, most likely, you are not absolutely sure, and your answer, whatever it may be, doesn't change the fact that you're here, right now, does it? It all seems a bit strange, but it's true. It's happening this very moment.

When I arrived at Ray's house that Friday night, I didn't expect anything different than any other Friday night. You know how those weekends go, right? A routine so tightly rehearsed, you could set time by it, give or take a few minutes; and like clockwork, Ray was sitting in front of the television rolling a joint and watching cartoons.

"Honey, I'm home. Where are the kids?," I asked, making my way into the kitchen.

Ray laughed at the television and ignored me, but I wasn't surprised in the least. I grabbed a beer from the refrigerator and drank it where I stood, scanning over all the notes and coupons in between gulps, when I noticed a corner of a nearly hidden photograph peeking out beyond a hand-written, chicken enchilada recipe. I plucked the photo off of the refrigerator door and flashed back to a prepubescent summer.

"Hey, come watch this, dude. It's a riot," Ray said, chuckling.

I held a photograph of four, grade school boys, each of them holding a fish in one hand and a fishing pole in the other, posing for the picture. Their sunbaked faces smiling at the camera, and an old Chevy truck and three tents rested in the background. I remembered the moment that photograph was taken, and the more I looked into those innocent faces, the heavier my heart felt. I recalled walking back to camp that day. Charlie had caught two fish that afternoon, because out of the four of us, he was the only one who actually knew how to use a fishing pole. I guess the rest of us were just lucky, except for

Ray. Moments before the picture was taken, Charlie handed Ray a fish to hold for the picture, so Ray wouldn't be the only one of us standing empty-handed. After the picture was taken, Ray returned the fish to Charlie and walked off, but Charlie called his name. When Ray looked back, Charlie tossed Ray the fish, which almost ended up landing in the dirt and said, "Now, we all can say we caught a fish."

Just about then, our skinny, rat-looking friend, Crumbs walked in with a 6-pack of Coors in hand. If you're wondering how he got his nickname, I already told you, but I'll tell you again. It's because he has very pointy facial features, resembling a rat. See, one afternoon, after finishing a bag of nacho cheese-flavored, Dorito chips, he poured the crumbs into his cupped hand and continued eating. When he had finished, he looked up and saw us staring at him.

"What? What's wrong?," he said, wrinkling his nose.

We all looked at each other, not saying a word.

Again, he asked, "What's up? What are you guys looking at? I got something on my face?"

Charlie looked at him and said, "You look like a rat, especially with that cheese dust on your nose."

We all broke in to laughter, all except Crumbs, and since we couldn't nickname him "Rat," we nicknamed him the next best thing, and that's how he got his name.

"Look at us. Even then, you could tell we were destined for greatness. Look at us; we caught fish. That's badass, man. Want a beer?," he sarcastically asked, sliding one into my jacket pocket and bumping me out of the way.

As Ray shouted for us to come smoke a joint, the phone rang.

"Don't answer it, dude. I'm serious," Ray insisted.

"Hello? Who's calling?," I asked, using my most prim and proper voice. "Wholly, shit, dude! I hope this isn't your only phone call."

I noticed Crumbs helping himself to a couple of prescription bottles near the coffee pot. He turned around and smiled and put two more pills in his pocket.

"Who is it, Jack?," Ray asked, walking into the kitchen and swiping a prescription bottle out of Crumbs's hand. "Dude, those are my dad's, for his muscle spasms, for his back. He must've forgotten them. Did you take any?"

As Charlie spoke into one ear, I bent the other for Crumbs's answer.

"They're for muscle spasms, like muscle relaxers?," Crumbs asked.

"Yeah. Did you pocket any? Don't

fucking lie either."

"No, dude. I'm sure; come on, man. They're for your dad. I was just reading the label."

Ray eyed him, trying to determine if Crumbs was telling the truth.

"Want a beer?," Crumbs asked, gently stabbing one into Ray's chest, as if it were a dagger. "I stabbed you with a beer, right between your titties. Soft and flabby."

"Fuck off," he said, popping the cap and taking a drink. "And, who's that? Charlie?"

I nodded.

"I swear that guy must have telepathy or something. He always knows when my parents are gone for the weekend," Ray said, moving closer to the phone. "Hey, Charlie, don't even ask to use my house for a party. I still remember the last time. Everyone tracked mud into the house, and I had to pay to have the carpets cleaned and not one stripper showed up, not a single one, Charlie. So, forget it. Don't even ask; plus, you still owe for the cleaning bill, dude."

Charlie laughed so loud that I had to pull the phone away from my ear. Ray finished his beer, helped himself to another one, took a hit off the joint, and walked back into the living room with a loud and dismissive burp. Crumbs sniffed the air and followed the smoke trail out of the kitchen.

When I hung up the phone, I had directions to Charlie's new address and an invitation to party in San Francisco; the only catch was, we had to leave within 15 minutes, because road time tacked on an hour, and time was ticking. Crumbs's eyes filled with excitement when I told him of Charlie's offer. He reminded me of a dog being asked if he'd like to go on a walk. Cigarette smoke swirled around his long teeth and escaped out the corners of his smiling mouth. "Enough said. What are we waiting for?," he said, getting off of the couch. Ray, on the other hand, had traffic school the following morning, and he couldn't afford to be absent. He had no other choice but to take a pass.

"Are you guys really leaving?," he questioned, already knowing the answer.

"You could have the last two beers, dude," Crumbs offered as a consolation.

And with that, Crumbs and I walked toward the front door, but Crumbs backtracked and darted into the kitchen for his beers, saying, "I changed my mind, dude; we're gonna need these for the ride." And as he closed the door, I heard Crumbs say, "Later, bator."

CHAPTER 2

We made our way north, taking I-280 toward San Francisco in Crumbs old, brown Nova. And to be honest about his car, it was a piece of shit. There's no denying it. Ever since the first day he showed up driving that thing, I always thought it looked a turd on four wheels; and to make matters worse, recently, someone felt the urge to snap his antenna and smash the rear, passenger window. But sitting shotgun, it really didn't matter how his car looked. I was more concerned with us making it to Charlie's without any car drama. You know what I mean, right? I just wanted to get there without breaking down on the side of the freeway, like sitting ducks, waiting for a highway patrol to "help" us.

"What's that smell?," I asked, looking about the car, then at the bottom of my shoes.

"I don't smell anything?," Crumbs answered without concern.

"You can't smell that? Are you serious, dude? It smells like a fucking locker room in here, like moldy towels and sweaty socks, like you wiped your ass with a wet rag, dude. Light a cigarette. Hey, just to let you know, there's fucking mold growing in here, man. Somewhere in the backseat, maybe, under the mats."

"Oh, that smell. Yeah, it's because it rained the other night, and I forgot to put plastic over the window in the back, so yeah. You're probably right."

"You forgot?"

"Well, not really, I taped a plastic bag to the door, but that shit blew off on my way to work, then it rained, so I said fuck it. I'll park in the sun and let nature dry it out. I don't even smell it anymore. Let's smoke a joint."

As we smoked, Crumbs laughed, and the broken window and moldy smell wasn't mentioned again. It was obvious that he didn't care, and why should he, who really sits in the backseat of his own car, so why worry about it? We talked and joked and then we didn't. We sat there stoned listening to the static-laced music, until it had become pure static. Crumbs turned off the radio. The sound of the Nova's retreaded tires speeding on the freeway filled the interior, and the soft, green glow from the dashboard lights, partially lit his face.

"Yeah, they broke the antenna, too. I wanna ask you something," Crumbs said, with half-massed eyes, tossing the roach into the ashtray.

Crumbs spoke about thoughts of enrolling in a trade school, moving forward in life, making money to move out of his widowed mother's home, but worried of leaving her behind. He mentioned several possibilities for a career path. I knew he was on the right track. You see, Ray, Crumbs, Charlie, and I were at the same point in our lives. We had no real prospects ahead, nothing concrete, no true foundation to build our futures on. Crumbs was right.

We should've decided our paths three or four years ago, but we didn't, because we were quite comfortable. I'm not saying that we didn't often discuss our futures, of course, we did. I mean, most friends do, right? We talked about doing this and doing that, going here and there, and how we were never going get old and crusty. But, that conversation always ended the same way each time: all of us quietly reflecting on what was said and passing a joint around. Honestly, none of us really took each other seriously, because we didn't take ourselves seriously. We kept keeping on the only way we knew how. Taking each day as it came.

"So, what do you think? Is it stupid or what, Jack?," Crumbs asked, looking at me for an answer.

"I think it's a good idea, man," I said, turning toward the window.

"You're not just saying that, are you? I know how you are, dude. Fucking lie to people to make them feel smarter than they really are. You fucking, tricky bastard. I can see you laughing inside. When you gonna stop selling? I know you've thought about it, and I know you make good money, but it can't last forever. Hate to see you get caught, you know. Shooting you straight right now, so don't take it the wrong way."

"Is that so wrong?," I asked, looking back at Crumbs.

"What? What I'm saying?"

"No, not that. I'm talking about occasionally hiding the truth from people," I said, turning more toward Crumbs.

"Occasionally? Come on, Jack. That sounds like bullshit."

"I'm not talking between friends, like you and me, but, you know, like most people, like people you really don't care about, you know, like your coworkers and shit. You know what I mean."

"On occasion?," Crumbs asked, then smirked.

"Right. On occasion."

Crumbs paused a moment and said, "Oh, those people. You mean, nobodies? Fuck'em. Fuck on occasion. Fucking lie to them all you want, all the time. Who really cares? I'm sure they lie to you. They don't care about you, right, so fuck'em. Who cares? I'm asking about me, Jacky. Don't lie to me. Do you think it's time I do something with my life or what?"

"Honest?"

"Dude, I'm gonna kill you. Yes, honest! Shit, man… you know what, fuck it. Nevermind. You're impossible, dude. I can totally fucking kill you right now. I should've known better. We're way too high to be talking about this shit. 'On occasion' and all your other bullshit. I don't even know what that means. I don't even know what I'm saying right now. See, Jacky, you're a tricky bastard, just like I said. You got me all twisted up like a pretzel, dude. Forget I even mentioned it."

Watching Crumbs lose control had me in hysterics. I couldn't remember the last time I laughed so hard, and he was right. We were way too stoned to be talking about serious life shit, but I had the answer to his question. I just had to catch my breath.

"This is the exit, right? This one, right?

Jack! Dude!"

"Yes, yes, this one," I said, feeling my stomach tighten again.

"Fuck! We're gonna miss it!"

Crumbs hit the brakes and yanked the steering wheel to the right. The car skidded into a small puddle of water and fishtailed off the freeway and into the exit lane as if it were planned.

"Okay, we're looking for the Flaming Bough Apartments. Charlie said to pull into the third driveway on the right, pass the pool and park next to the two dumpsters," I instructed, still chuckling. "And, yeah, you should. Time's ticking for all of us. Honest."

Without looking at me, Crumbs smiled, waited a moment and said, "Thanks, Jacky. I love you, man. You know that, right? But, dude, you really got some fucking serious issues going on up there."

"Yeah, I know. Now, park the fucking car, son," I said, laughing as I pinched his earlobe.

CHAPTER 3

The Flaming Bough Apartments were nothing more than two-story, cement boxes with windows. Someone thought of adding overgrown bushes and small patches of dead grass to the grounds to lessen the effects of depression. The parking lot had some lights, but they were either blown out, facing the wrong direction, or flickering away to their death. Either way, it all made no difference to us.

"Man, look at this shithole," Crumbs whispered, as we walked deeper into the apartment complex. Charlie lived in building D, first floor, so after ten minutes of walking, we heard a familiar voice jumping out of a small, well-lit room, "Goddamn it. It never fails. They're damp."

We entered the laundry room, taking

witness to Charlie talking to the white machine. "You're a dryer, aren't you?," he questioned, then smacked its face. "Then act like one. Dry my clothes, you fucking thief." Charlie looked thinner and a bit taller. Something was different about him. His dirty-blond hair lost most of its golden hue. It now just looked short and dirty. The coarse mustache hairs curled beyond his upper lip, so now when he smiled, the black lines from his porcelain crowns, which the dentist constructed to replace Charlie's front teeth, were hidden. Only a sliver of teeth peeked out from his hairs.

"You guys made it. Shit. There's hope for you yet. I need some quarters. These damn machines are worse than playing the fucking slots. At least with the slots, you have a chance at winning. These things just take your money and give you damp clothes in return and then got the balls to ask you for more money. What else are you going to do? Wear wet clothes? Am I right or what?," Charlie asked, bouncing on the balls of his feet with excitement.

"You look good, man. Check out that hair," Crumbs said, handing Charlie some change.

"The crazy thing about it is, you give it to them. They're like bullies asking for your milk money. Choke on it," Charlie said, feeding more quarters to the dryer, then gave it a swift kick in the belly. "Let's get out of here."

Charlie led us back to his apartment. His place was a small, one bedroom with a futon in the living room, another futon in the bedroom, a kitchen table and three miss-match chairs. The television sat on a blue, milk crate and only supported two, local stations. One English. One Spanish. Charlie had decorated the walls with artwork, the type of artwork that sells well on street corners, cheap, metal frames included. To be honest, I actually expected more from Charlie, but who was I to talk, I was unemployed, didn't own a car, and still lived with my folks.

"I like it. What do you think, Jack? It's roomy. Lots of space, just how I like it. Man, you could really fix this place up. All you really need is a better couch, a few better pictures, some chairs that match, which you can easily find and maybe a…." Crumbs said, as if he was on the verge of renting it.

I watched Crumbs mince about the living room and loved his optimistic bullshit. Bullshitting was Crumbs's hidden talent. Man, if you gave him enough time, that guy could make you feel good about any fucked up situation. He'd convince you that your lost cat or dog is better off now, because the animal is not truly lost; it's actually free, because all animals, by nature's law, were intended to live freely. I mean, did you think nature intended for birds and monkeys to live in cages, whales to live in captivity and perform stupid tricks for amusement? And, we all know how tigers and elephants feel about doing too many shows on any given day, especially the tigers.

You know, I bet, right now, your cat or dog is doing just fine. Trust me. I understand. That's not to say, that you're not concerned. Of course, you are. It's only natural for you to be concerned, right? I mean, you guys spent a lot of time together, and I understand that you'll miss that. But what you really should be concerned about are the cats and dogs that are not doing fine. Right now, they're waiting for someone like you, an animal lover, to save them, and I know one of those guys would love to spend the rest of its life with you…. And, chances are Crumbs would accompany that person down to the local animal shelter and help pick out a new cat or dog for that person. He made an art out of bullshitting people and loved it.

"Cut the crap. This place is a dump, Crumbs. I know it, but, hey, it works for me at this moment in my life, so fuck it. You gotta know when to say fuck it, you know, and this is one of those times. What do you say we go downtown and get us some drinks, lots of drinks?," Charlie asked.

Those were the magic words: lots of drinks. Within minutes, we were out the door and walking to the Chevy. Crumbs produced a thick, brown blanket and a plastic trash bag from the trunk and laid them across the backseat for me. I was given the special treatment.

CHAPTER 4

The evening air felt brisk and made its way through the broken window in the rear. Charlie talked about plans of starting a small business. Charlie read a newspaper article the other day about this guy who made a small fortune selling trinkets to tourists.

"I could write slogans, all kinds of them, funny ones, stupid ones, print famous quotes, you know, and make money doing it. Maybe, even open up a small shop on the wharf and sell them to all the fucking tourists around here, all fucking daylong. Cash money, son," Charlie said, flicking his cigarette's ashes out of the window.

Crumbs agreed, but I kept myself out of the conversation. I didn't have anything to add to the conversation; and, just between you and I, I didn't give a shit. It's sad, but true. I figured,

"Hell, if you want take a shot at something, who am I to say anything? Go ahead. Be my fucking guest. It's your money, not mine." Risk is like anything else in life. Sometimes, you win and sometimes you lose. It's how you win and lose that makes the real difference. That's the truth, and the $200 bucks in my pocket backed it up.

When they asked for my thoughts, I simply agreed without concern. I was too busy thinking of moving to San Francisco, getting out of the neighborhood, and starting fresh. San Francisco felt like a different world. Colorful neon glowed along the streets, all the different colors streaking together, beauty to my eyes, until the glaring, oncoming headlights struck me, blinding me for a moment, as the Chevy's tires chirped and squealed with each turn.

"There's one, take it or we'll lose it. Parking's like gold here," Charlie said, pointing across the street.

Crumbs hit the brakes and flipped a U-turn in the middle of the street and squeezed in between a graffiti-painted delivery truck and a green, Ford sedan. The Chinese restaurant, a few feet down, hustled with customers. As we stepped onto the street, we heard the car's engine rumble with pings and knocks, knowing Crumbs always goes for the cheapest gas he could buy. Most of the stores were closed for the night, and only a few panhandlers crept along the street.

The air held the aroma of greasy chow mein, cigarettes and green-bud marijuana. Everything around me found its place in my short-term memory.

"Okay, this it is: The Gold Digger," Charlie said, crossing the street onto the next block. Crumbs held open the door and smiled, as we entered the bar beneath its blue and yellow neon marquee.

A 1950's jukebox played Wilson Picket's *Mustang Sally*. Red carpet covered half of the floor and cheap, black and white tiles covered the other half. The plastic tiles reminded me of a grade-school classroom floor, well worn and easy to clean. The place smelled of cigarettes, stale beer, and drug store perfume. Most of the patrons, hunched at the bar, didn't pay us any mind.

However, the two women, who sat closest to the jukebox, smiled as though we were dinner. Nearby, some guys gathered around the pool table, like pigeons waiting for breadcrumbs. A few other people sat at two-person tables, drinking and talking and getting on with their evening. It was all very normal, except for Christina, the bartender.

"These your friends, Charlie?," she asked, uncapping three beers. Crumbs and I selected the barstools flanking Charlie's.

"Well, hello, to you, too. This here is Crumbs and that's Jack. He'll whisper sweet words into your ears and make you feel warm and tingly and try to squeeze every drop of love right out of you."

She smiled and the introductions were properly sealed with handshakes and drinks from our beers.

Christina's hands felt rough, and her light blue fingernail polish needed a new coat. Her black, stretch denim pants outlined her best assets, especially when walking to serve the two women at the end of the bar. There was no denying her hips had a seductive sway and her ass had just the right amount of jiggle. Her customers knew it and so did she. But, it was her lingering perfume that kept me reeling.

Time passed without notice, as it so often does when drinking with friends. Charlie, red-faced and breath stinking of booze, continued talking of plans for making money. He mentioned something about inventing a gadget for fishing boats and told us that this gadget would dominate the market, and we wouldn't need to work real jobs. It was foolproof, as he put it. Crumbs became so enthralled with the talk of making money, wearing fancy clothes, and all that, that he bought the next two rounds; we were all going to be business partners. I must admit, the dream sounded great, and at that moment, we were tighter than a pair of Speedos on a fat guy's ass. It was the three of us against the world, and we loved the odds. Crumbs threw back his shot, turned to Charlie, then to me, and rose off his barstool and strutted over to the big jukebox with laughable swagger.

While he stood at the glowing jukebox, one of the women sitting at the end of the bar approached Charlie with a smile. She introduced herself to us and then focused her attention on Charlie. He didn't waste any time turning on his charm. She wore a gray sweater that snugged her tightly and exposed her mid-drift. Her black boots matched her Spandex miniskirt. She reminded me of one of those print models, the ones you see posing in department store ads, the ones selling curtains, blenders, skillets, any basic household item. Don't get me wrong; she was pretty, and I would have settled for her or any other woman in the place, but she wasn't pretty enough to go big time. Paris, London, and New York weren't calling. She was more along the lines of Fresno and Bakersfield. She had the perfect look for selling hair dye and conditioner.

Crumbs buzzed around and picked up a broken piece of chalk and scribbled his name on the chalkboard, next to the pool stick rack. His name sat below some guy named Manuelito. Using the large mirror behind the bar, I noticed Crumbs swagger over to the remaining woman at the end of the bar. She watched, as her friend laughed with Charlie and cozied up to him, but when Crumbs sat down next to her, all of her attention shifted to Crumbs. As Charlie listened to the woman sitting next to him, he nodded to Christina, indicating it was time for another round, a Manhattan for her, a Screwdriver for him, and a vodka and cranberry for me.

Crumbs looked at me and smiled from the end of the bar, as the woman headed for the restroom. Her thick ass bounced from left to right as she walked. Crumbs flicked his tongue at the chick's shifting thickness, and I laughed and he smiled again, and we returned to our drinks. When his named was called from the pool table, he ignored it, as any right-minded man would do. It was obvious that he was playing a different sort of game.

Truthfully, my ass had nearly gone numb from sitting so long and my bladder had reached its capacity, so I peeled myself from the barstool and walked to the restroom with a slight sway. Small, black and white tiles covered the floor and the urinals, toilets, and sinks looked very old. I stepped toward the wall that supported the three urinals and chose the one that had something scribbled above it. The wall-carving read: "For good head, call Sally." While I pissed, I looked up at the words again and noticed that someone had crossed out the "ly" in Sally and wondered if Sally and Sal were the same person. Lou Reed's *Take a Ride on the Wild Side* played in my mind. I washed my hands and returned to my barstool.

There was a guy with a furry scarf sitting on the barstool next to mine. When I sat down and lit a smoke, he asked for one, which was fine. I mean, I didn't have a reason not to share cancer with a stranger, but he took the cigarette as an invitation to start a conversation.

CHAPTER 5

The middle-aged stranger with an unshaven, double-chin, a gap between his front teeth and a maroon colored, leather jacket spoke about general, mundane things, like the weather and how much he enjoyed the city and how welcoming it is to people like him. As he rambled on, I noticed that he held his cigarette in between this middle and ring fingers. "Thanks for the smoke, guy," he said and took a drag. "I'm Marty. I'll tell you, man, it feels good to have a drink and forget about life for a while...."

Marty spewed woes of his crumby desk job, sputtering sex life, and failed attempt at learning bass guitar. I smoked my cigarette, made smoke rings, and nodded in agreement, as if I actually gave two shits. Crumbs and Charlie chatted with the two women, and I ordered another shot. "It's on the house, honey," Christina said, with a tinge of pity. Pressing a smile, I tossed two bucks on the counter, returned to blowing smoke rings, and surrendered to the moment. She scooped up the tip and stuffed the bills into a mason jar that rested next to the cash register. I threw back the shot and ordered a vodka and tonic. Booze and cigarettes danced on my tongue, like two lovers holding each other in a tight embrace, melding into a colorful blur of tango. Marty said something, smiled, and another drink appeared from Christina's hand, and that type of magic continued.

After the fourth free drink, Marty felt lubed enough to tell me about his ex-wife, Jeanne. She lived in Tallahassee, and his son recently moved to Las Vegas. He paused while a sadden expression unfolded over his face. One of his personal demons kicked open the door to his thoughts. I pretended not to notice.

"Steven. My son," he said. "He doesn't return my calls anymore. Am I wrong to expect him to understand?," he questioned, staring into his glass, as though he had forgotten that I was even there. He remained quiet for a long while, not saying a single word. His thoughts having their way with him in some dark corner of his mind. We drank in silence and exercised our spirits accordingly.

After another drink and cigarette, Marty shook my hand and said, "Our lives are never truly our own, Jack, even if we believe them to be. Life is a spider web." He wished me a good evening and walked out of the bar and into the night. A few inches from my hand, Marty's glass sat alone and empty.

The once lively chattering had now dwarfed to a low murmur. Only a few pigeons pecked at the pool table, and several names remained abandoned on the chalkboard. However, next to the pool stick rack, the middle-aged couple groping each other caught my eye. The chubby, blond-haired woman with her black roots showing sat pinned against the wall, legs spread on a barstool. She puffed on her cigarette, as her guy nuzzled into her, kissing her neck and kneading her doughy love handles. They were comfortably lost in their romantic drunkenness. Her eyelids fluttered slowly like the wings of a dying butterfly. I watched with bewildered amusement; and when her eyes widen enough to noticed me observing her, her rum-soaked voice cackled and subsided in to a smoker's cough. Embarrassment slapped my face and forced me to turn away.

Charlie turned to me and helped himself to a smoke while Ms. gray sweater wandered off toward the restroom. She smiled at her friend and Crumbs as she passed them and disappeared behind the thick-painted restroom door. Charlie sucked his teeth and mumbled, "I'm getting some of that tonight; there's no doubt, brother. You know what I'm saying, fucker?," he asked, smiling devilishly. Feigning to be mad, I pretended to deliver a punch to his jaw. He exaggerated my strength and made his eyes roll about in his sockets. We laughed like two drunken brothers. "She's the lucky one, man," I offered. Charlie didn't immediately respond; he just looked at me for a moment, as one does when inspecting something for an estimated value. He broke a small, humble smile and threw an arm around my shoulders and squeezed, until nearly knocking me off my barstool.

When Ms. gray sweater returned from doing her pat, pat, front to back business, her lips were glossed redder than before. Her refreshed perfume indicated her engine was still running.

She sat down, saying, "Sorry, I stole Charlie from you. But, it looks like your other friend is having fun." She lifted her eyebrows, held them for a moment, and giggled.

"Don't apologize. Nothing risked, nothing gained, right?"

"Good. You guys talk. I got to see a man about a horse," Charlie said, peeling himself from his barstool and staggering off toward the urinals. She started a conversation about the bar and something else, and mentioned something about her fat cat and it's annoying hairballs, which caused her to laugh and carry on. I nodded and yawned, imagining a fat, orange cat coughing up hairballs and randomly pissing and shitting in Charlie's apartment.

Charlie returned with a refreshed look on his face, as though he just snorted a line or two. He appeared happily content with the way things were going. "Christina, one more round, please," he insisted. "Last one, it's closing time, babe," she answered, and dinged the brass bell, signaling her customers to come and get them. The last of the revelers drifted to the bar while others staggered for the door. Joyful slurred speech followed. Christina merely smiled and fetched their drinks. She pulled a bottle of Irish whiskey and poured us departing shots. Crumbs smiled and showed us his reddish gums and long teeth.

The five of us sat at the bar, like two pairs and a jack. Christina raised her shot glass and said, "To the good times," and threw back the booze. "It was nice meeting you guys. Now, it's time to leave. I want to go home." As Charlie whispered into Ms. gray sweater's ear, I whispered into his, "The booze is going right through me. I'll be right back; don't go anywhere."

"Go take a piss," he slurred, lifting a flaming match to his cigarette.

In front of the same urinal as earlier, I unzipped, conducted my business, and cocked it to the right side of my pants before zipping up. As I pulled the chrome handle to flush, Lou

Reed's lyrics entered my head again, and the room started spinning. I bumped my way into the stall and sat down on the toilet, hoping to regain my balance. I rested for a few minutes and stood up. My hair felt oily; my eyes stung a bit, and my long-winded fart was left behind, as I walked out of the restroom.

The bar was darker than some time before and completely empty, except for Christina, who was startled when she saw me walking out of the restroom.

"Jesus Christ! You scared the shit out of me, man. Fucking aye, I didn't know you were still here," she said, watching me.

"Sorry, I'm sorry. I think I passed out or something," I admitted, feeling as if I had done something wrong.

"They're outside waiting for you," she said, but her tone made her words sound, as if she said, "Dude, get the fuck out of here. I don't really know you, and I don't have a problem calling the cops."

She darted out from behind the bar and ushered me to the door and out into the cold night. Before I could say goodnight, I heard the door close and the dead bolt lock behind me. Fog drifted just above storefront roofs, and all was quiet.

CHAPTER 6

The evening air swooshed up and bit my face and continued moving up the street, as if it was waiting for me the entire time. In the distance, a few glowing headlights disappeared into the fog. Christina was wrong: they weren't waiting for me outside. There was no sign of Charlie and Crumbs. They were gone. I figured that they were waiting in the car, so I crossed the street over to the next block. When I turned the corner, the parking space where Crumbs had parked his car was empty. I stared at the empty space in disbelief. "No fucking way," I whispered under my breath. "This shit ain't happening."

Choosing to believe that Crumbs and Charlie were playing a practical joke on me, I wandered about hoping to hear Charlie's recognizable laughter. Not knowing what else to do, I continued walking up the street. I scanned the rows of parked cars, but Crumb's car was nowhere to be found. A pair of headlights approached, almost blinding me, yet I hopefully stared into them, but the car drove passed me and disappeared. There wasn't a single Chevy Nova on the street. And against my willingness to believe, I knew in my heart that Charlie and Crumbs were gone, leaving me stranded in San Francisco. The only thing I had going for me was the $106.00 in my pocket. I kept walking for no other reason but to keep moving. I had to keep moving. I imagined those bastards driving up next to me, laughing their asses off, and yelling for me to jump in the car, but it was only my imagination keeping hope alive.

I had walked a solid twenty minutes when an unfamiliar voice made itself known.

"Hey, man, you alright? You look lost or something. You lost?," the voice asked. A guy wearing an Oakland Raiders cap and brown windbreaker stepped out of the dark.

"Nope," I shot back, and kept walking. "I ain't lost."

San Francisco takes on a different persona after the sun has fallen below the horizon; and like slimy, crunchy creatures that live easier in the dark than the light, there are people who only take to the streets under a darkened sky. The stranger in the cap and windbreaker trailed some feet behind me, as though I didn't notice.

"What are you looking for, man? Maybe, I can help you out. Maybe, I got what you're looking for. There's a lot to be found in the Tenderloin. Man, you don't even know where you're going. The way you're looking over your shoulders and shit and trying to eye every car that drives by. Shit, man, you're lost and you know it, and so do I," he said, jogging up besides me. "Just tell me what's wrong and maybe I can help you out. Name's Teddy, just like the singer. What's yours?"

"Thanks, but it's all under control, man," I said, trying to sound fearless and wondering of his reason for following me.

I continued walking, as if I knew my exact direction while attempting to put distance between us. The last thing I wanted was to confirm Teddy's suspicion of me: I was a lost and drunk guy from the suburbs.

"Hey, you like Teddy Pendergrass?"

"Who? No, don't know the guy."

"Check it out. *You got, you got, you got what I want. You got, you got, you got what I need.* Now, do you know Teddy Pendergrass? He's motherfucking old school, man. Don't tell me you don't know," he said, looking directly at me, as though I came from a different planet.

He appeared beyond confused that I never heard of Teddy Pendergrass, the R&B singer.

Actually, when I turned away from his piercing stare, I thought this guy is fucking crazy, and he won't stop following me. I must get away from him, and I shouldn't say anything bad about Teddy Pendergrass, whoever he was.

"Man, I never met anybody, not anyone, who has never heard of Teddy Pendergrass. He's fucking famous, like a motherfucker. He's one of the reasons why so many women got pregnant in the '70's and 80's. I'm damn sure of that. If you don't think so, just listen to *Turn Off The Lights*. That song alone will get any woman, any motherfucking woman with ears on her damn head pregnant. It's like he gets them pregnant with his voice. I mean, any dude, all they need to do is put on *Turn Off The Lights* and let that motherfucker sing for a minute, and there you go. His woman will be ready for the picking, you know, what I'm saying?"

He acted as if we were longtime friends, rambling on and sharing his personal and intimate thoughts with me; and although, I wished that he would disappear, I must admit, he had my attention. I kept walking, and he kept talking.

"Now, Barry White, he's the other dude that gets women pregnant with his voice. But, I prefer Teddy, because he's got that confident swagger about him, like when he's singing all that sweet, romantic shit, getting the chicks wet and tingling, he's really saying, 'Look, girl, I'm not trying to get you pregnant here, but if I do, I mean, with my music and all, I know you won't mind. This will always be our song, girl.' Then, he would sing *Close The Door* and, when the song ends, they're pregnant. It's real simple. You understand, right? Hey, man, you got a cigarette you can spare?"

When stopping under a streetlight to hand Teddy a smoke, I noticed his jaundice-colored eyes, then the long scar on the left side of his head. The thin, white scar stretched from above his left ear to below his jawline. His scar looked like a long, spaghetti noodle stuck to his face. I felt the need to ask how he received the scar, but decided against it. It wasn't my business. I just wanted him to stop following me, so I turned and quickened my pace, hoping he'd take the hint.

On the steps of a nearby apartment building, a couple sat smoking a pipe. The lighter's streaming flame cast an orange glow against their haggard faces each time the pipe switched hands. "Slow. Hit it slow or you're going to burn it all up, bitch," the man hissed at the dirty-faced woman, as I passed the couple. I continued walking, losing track of time, and realized that Teddy didn't get the hint. He remained a relaxed pace or two behind me, casually smoking his cigarette, appearing as if he was taking a stroll through the park on a Sunday afternoon.

I knew it didn't make much sense walking without direction and knew that I had no real chance of finding Crumbs and Charlie, but for some strange reason, I kept walking and it made me feel better about my unfortunate situation. As futile as it may have been, I felt as though I was doing my part to be found, staying awake and drifting though the night. My feet were beginning to tire, and Teddy kept pace with me again. I believe Teddy had a fear of silence, because he started rambling again about this and that, a bunch of unrelated topics crisscrossing over each other, one after another, but I didn't say anything about it. I figured he was truly crazy and had nothing better to do with his time. I'm sure I wasn't the first stranger he attached himself to that night, and he would eventually break off and disappear. Besides, when roaming the streets at night, two persons are better than one, so I listened to what Teddy had to say. What other choice did I have? I learned that Teddy moved from Alabama to San Francisco at the age of 10 and had lived in most of the city's districts. Until recently, he worked as a longshoreman in Oakland, but was fired for testing positive for a controlled substance. He swore that he would still be employed if that damn company didn't conduct random drug testing.

"Man, those motherfuckers didn't know shit for the longest time. I'd show up and do my time, every motherfucking day. What more do they want? So what if I like getting high. I still do my job, and I do it good. You hear me? I wasn't starting no static with nobody, and I was making good money, too. 12 duckets an hour with benefits. Shit, man, those were some good days," Teddy said, drifting into his past for a moment.

"Man, okay, I ain't gonna lie, I was doing more shit than I should have, but that was my business, you know? Then, I got paranoid, couldn't sleep, didn't eat too much, jacking off all the time, motherfucking pornos. I used to buy them at this little Chinese store by my old apartment," he chuckled and looked at me, then chuckled again. "Yeah, man, I was tripping, so I talked to my friend about it, and he told he had this special mixture, some detox shit. Man, that shit was so nasty. It burned my throat bad. I couldn't really talk, only whisper for two days after I drank that shit. He said it would detox my system. That motherfucker bullshitted me, man. He just went into his dirty-ass kitchen and started grabbing shit in his cupboards, spices and shit, and squeezing lemons and hot sauce, and motherfucking raw eggs. He even made me buy some spice called cumin and some yellow powder shit. I drank like a gallon of that junk and, man, I couldn't stop pissing and shitting for two days straight. I was afraid to leave the house. I thought that dude poisoned me or something, couldn't even talk, sweating all the time. Man, I called that son-of-a-bitch up and was like, 'What the hell, man?' And he said, 'The stuff is doing its job. Don't worry. Keep drinking it,' and hung up. Even after all that stupid bullshit, my test still came back positive. Can you believe that shit, man?"

Beads of sweat collected on my brow and my back felt hot and moist and my feet throbbed. I stopped walking and faced Teddy and asked, "Do you have a car?" My vision blurred and my stomach flipped over. I turned away and vomited into the street. Everything swayed back and forth. I held onto a signpost for fear of falling. Teddy said something, which sounded more like grunting than actual words. I closed my eyes and held on tighter. I floated in darkness, spinning out of control, and the cold air felt good on my face. I surrendered trying to be found and let myself go, allowing the night to take me wherever it wanted. Deep breathes, dragging my sleeve across my mouth, and opening my eyes again. Teddy's warped and grunting sounds turned in to "Man, you alright? You're fucked up. Man, you alright?," he asked again.

"Yeah, I got a car, but it ain't got no gas. Why? You got money, how much?," he grunted.

"A few bucks. I could give you some if you drive me to a friend's house. It's around here."

"I don't know, man. Look, maybe, you need to--"

"I'll give you some money, okay? I just need to get out of here."

"Whatever you say, man. My ride's parked over here, in front of my partner's house, follow me."

As we walked toward Van Ness, my stomach cramped and pained me with each step, and my tongue felt so dry that it remained glued to the roof of my mouth. Whenever I tried speaking, my throat would involuntarily swallow and break my sentences in two. Teddy didn't notice when I choked on my words, because he was too busy walking and talking about his girlfriend, who enjoys ham sandwiches without mayonnaise and having sex in front of mirrors and in public places. We must have walked another 30 minutes or so before Teddy said that we were almost there. "My car's parked two blocks away," he said, trotting to the next block, pointing to an alley.

I followed, as though I were tethered to him, but stopped when Teddy headed for the alley.

"Man, you ain't gotta trip. This way's shorter. Come on. If you want a ride, you're gonna need to follow me to my car. It's this way," he said, disappearing into the alley.

His voice bounced off the walls and ricocheted out of the darkness. I could hardly see where he stood. Feigning courage, I stepped into the alley with only the orange glow of my lit cigarette to guide me. The strong scent of urine and rotting garbage invaded my wet nostrils, as my pupils dilated and adjusted to the darkness. A high pitch rang in my ears.

"Teddy, where are you, man?," I questioned, entering deeper into the darkness. I felt something move close to me.

"Right here, motherfucker."

Pain flooded the back of my head and pops of white light followed me to the ground. Feet shuffled about, as I was struck again with something other than a fist. "I'm going to die in this alley," I thought. "I'm going to die tonight." My heart now beat in my ears and my throat, and the taste of blood reminded me of old pennies. I traded a kick to my stomach to get to my feet. For every two punches I threw into the dark, I received one good one. I moved about chaotically, like a fearful animal in a poacher's cage. I couldn't see Teddy, but I could hear his angry voice, "Go down motherfucker. Go down. You're beat!" I was fighting a shadow in a lightening storm. "Just go down," he said, swinging something that cut through the air. Everything went black.

When I awoke, I saw Teddy standing over me smoking a cigarette. And each time he would take a drag, the orange glow would reflect off his glassy eyes and sweaty face. I tried to say something, but choked on blood. The cigarette's glow disappeared, and everything went black again. His footsteps trotted away and faded into the darkness, as if he was never there. On my back, I laid in the dark alley, feeling my racing heartbeat slow down, beat by beat, but the ringing in my ears and the taste of blood continued.

CHAPTER 7

After a minute or two, I ran my fingers over the egg-shaped bump on the back of my head. It felt hot and throbbed, but there wasn't any blood. I checked my chest and stomach for knife wounds and found none. My pockets were empty. Teddy robbed me of everything; all of my money was gone; the son of a bitch even stole my cigarettes. I crawled to the nearby wall and rested against it. The cold cement wall cooled me and felt good. As I sat hunched over and with my back literally up against the wall, a pair of headlights approached. I tucked myself into a ball, much like a spider does the moment before getting crushed.

The sound of the car's V8 engine compressed and grew louder within the alley walls, as the car zoomed toward me, and its headlights bounced with each found pothole.

The driver blinded me with white lights, and there was nothing I could do, except close my eyes and turn my head. The driver downshifted through the gears, dropping rpms, and stepped on the brakes. The car skidded a bit, crept along side of me, and stopped. I tried crawling away, but it was too late. The passenger rolled down the window.

"Are you alright, honey? Looks like you need a ride to the emergency room. Do you want a ride?," the squeaky female voice asked from inside the car's interior.

"No. I'm— no, I'm okay. I'm just— "

A second voice within the car asked, "Want a ride to a phone or somewhere? You look like hammered shit, sweetheart. You should really call someone." This voice was deeper than the first, but it still sounded like a woman's, somewhat, through the ringing in my ears.

"Let us give you a ride. Your nose is bleeding," the first voice said.

I agreed to her offer, because anything was better than sitting in some dark alley in San Francisco bleeding onto myself. "Thank you," I said, peeling myself from the wall and approaching the car.

When the car door opened, the interior dome light shined bright with hope, like a lighthouse on a stormy night, and caused me to squint a bit. A woman's high heel struck the ground hard, so I followed it up her leg. She had one leg on the ground and another inside the car and wore silver toe rings under fishnet stockings under a miniskirt. Her face and torso were nothing more than a silhouette with a voice. "What happened to your cute face?," the voice asked. She moved a little to one side to allow the light to shine on me.

"I slipped and fell down and bit my lip. Got a bloody nose. It's nothing really, just a few scratches. That's all," I garbled back, coughing and spitting out a glob of blood.

"You must've fallen pretty hard to get that gash on your eyebrow. Looks like you may need a stitch or more."

She was right. Just above my right eyebrow, I felt a burning sensation, painful and sticky to the touch. The odd thing about it was, I didn't feel the pain until she mentioned it.

"He can't be more than 22, 23 years old. What a shame, this fucking city. Do you need help getting in the car, sugar?," the huskier voice asked.

"It's okay; I'm just moving a little slow. Sorry," I said, moving closer. As my vision sharpened, I followed the woman's toe rings, up to her ankle, up to her calf, up to her knee, up to her thigh, stopped and turned away.

"What's wrong, darling? Not your cup of tea?," the passenger said, giggling and slightly shifted her knee inward. "You're not going to let a couple of oversized clits get in the way of getting a ride, are you?"

The driver chuckled at her friend's remark and lit a cigarette.

"I… I— shit, I mean, what? You're?"

"What? I'm sure you've been in a locker room before, haven't you, like in high school, college, wherever?"

"Yeah, but—"

"Well, there's a bunch of dicks flopping around in there, right? Bet you even took a shower in the locker room before, didn't you?"

"Yeah, but—"

"Did it bother you then?"

"No, but—"

"So, why are you going to let it bother you now, sweet cheeks?," the passenger asked, as she plucked the cigarette from her friend's hand, took a puff, and handed it back. "Well, what's your excuse, baby face? Dicks are dicks, right?"

"Yeah, I guess, but the guys in the locker room weren't wearing fishnets and miniskirts.

They chuckled then laughed. I wiped my nose on my sleeve and wondered if the driver's curly hair was real or a wig.

"Would you close the door, Giselle? The boy said he doesn't want a ride and it's getting late," the driver said. "I want to go to the club and see Xavier. Plus, I think these shoes are making my feet swell. The price we pay to be divas, most will never know. Close the door, girl. Time to go."

"You don't know what you're missing, cutie. But for your own sake, don't pass on the ride; at least, let us drop you off at a gas station or something."

"Thanks, anyway, but I'll be alright. Do you think I can I bum a smoke before you go, if it's okay?"

She pulled a pack from her purse and held out her white hand. "Are you sure you're fine?," she asked. "We won't do anything against your wishes, if that's what you're worried about. I promise."

I reached for the cigarette and the lighter and lit the smoke, inhaling deeply. My lungs expanded and my head spun and spun again. I became dizzy and tried to plant my hand on the car for stability, but I misjudged the distance and stumbled backwards a couple of steps until I fell on my ass. Shame and embarrassment washed over me. I picked up my cigarette and took another drag, knowing that I was in no condition to make it on my own. At the very least, I needed some other place than this piss stinking alley to recuperate, to get my shit together, and I wondered if Teddy would reappear.

"Yeah, I think I'll take you up on that ride," I said, then pulled a drag and flicked my cigarette farther into the alley.

Giselle stepped out of the car and, with a firm grip, helped me up and into the backseat. "See, now, that wasn't too hard, was it?," she said. Darkness surrounded me again, except for the green glow from the dashboard lights and the burning cherry from the driver's cigarette.

The cold, vinyl backseat soothed my aching back, and I closed my eyes and hoped for the best. I'd become a piece of driftwood floating in a nameless tributary stream. I soon discovered that the driver was named Alice, and she was madly in love with a guy named Xavier. She proclaimed her love for him several times and swore that they would live together before the end of the year or by next spring. Other than that, Alice didn't say too much. She just complained about her sore feet in between the choruses of Donna Summer's *Bad Girls* and left the rest of the conversation to Giselle.

"Here, honey, take this and apply pressure to your cut. It'll stop the bleeding," Giselle instructed. I opened my eyes and took the wad of tissue paper from her hand. "Before we go any farther, we should all be on first name basis, okay? I'm Giselle and that's Alice; she's not much of a talker. She's more of a doer, if you know what I mean," Giselle said, yielding a chuckle from Alice. "So, what should we call you, handsome?"

"Jack. My name is Jack."

"Okay, Jack," she said, in an exaggerated masculine tone. "What the hell happed to you, and don't give me that 'I slipped and fell' bullshit. Tell me what really happened. Who kicked your ass?" Her semi-shadowed face moved in for a closer inspection.

"You want the truth?"

"Uh, yeah, is that too much to ask? Hello, Jack? I'm listening."

"Some dude named Teddy kicked my ass. I don't know who he is or if his name is even Teddy for certain. Do you have any aspirins? My head won't stop throbbing."

Giselle repeated Teddy's name and searched through her purse. "Sorry, all I found is a joint and a flask of vodka. Is that okay?, she asked. She pulled out the joint, lit it up, and passed it around, then took a swig off the flask and handed it to Alice. Inhale. Exhale. Drink. Swallow. Pass. Repeat. It appeared as if Giselle enjoyed playing hostess.

"Well, aren't you going to ask where we're going? Or, do you think we're driving around the city picking up strays for kicks, Jeff?," Alice asked, making Giselle giggle.

"His name's not Jeff, Alice. It's Jack. Isn't that right, Jacky?"

"To tell you the truth, I'm just glad to be off the street. I really don't care where we're going."

"See, Giselle, he doesn't care where he's going. He said himself. I'm liking your attitude, Jeff," Alice said, smiling at me in the rearview mirror.

"Have you ever partied with drag queens, Jack? We're fantastic!"

Alice asked Giselle something, which made Giselle turn and look at me. She batted her long fake eyelashes at me in a flirting fashion, as she held in her hit. When I broke eye contact, she blew her hit in my face, giggled, and turned around.

"No, I can't say that I've ever hung out with trannies before. It's no big deal, really," I said, feigning cool confidence.

Giselle pulled down the sun visor and used the mirror to freshen her makeup. In the tiny mirror, I'd catch her making eyes at me, but I wasn't exactly certain, because of my current state of mind. When I turned away from her stare, she giggled in a way that reminded me of a flirty schoolgirl. She had an amusing and interesting nature about her. "Whatever," I thought. "Just play it like a piece of driftwood and go with the flow."

Alice talked to Giselle about things I didn't understand, so I tuned out and craned my head back, resting upon the top of the backseat, and stared out of the rear window and into the night. We drove under hidden stars, under the foggy sky, under countless white and colorful lights, moving fast, far beyond my understanding of it all. And when it became too much to think about, I inhaled and exhaled, until my hot breath overtook the cold glass with an opaque, human fog that blocked out my view to the outside world.

Alice told Giselle that I was her responsibility tonight, because she didn't want Xavier to have any misunderstanding about me. Giselle agreed without rebuttal. I sensed that we were approaching the club and began stating reasons to remain in the car. Giselle said that I need not worry about money, because they knew the doorman, and money wouldn't be a problem. I said that I didn't want to offend anyone with my battered appearance, but she offered to clean and Band-Aid my wounds and smoke another joint with me. She even showed me a near-full bottle of vodka she had stashed in her purse, so drinks weren't an issue either. Giselle seemed to have an answer for each of my excuses. However, I still tried backing out of entering the club.

Alice parked the car on a dimly lit, side street and freshened up her face. I confessed that the pain had returned, and it would be best if I remained in the car and tried to sleep. I even promised to be there when they returned. Alice stopped applying her lipstick, turned around, and said, "You'll be a lot safer in there than out here. Trust me, Jack. I'll give you some vicodin inside, but you're going to need to change that sloppy shirt. There's a plastic bag back there with some clothes in it. Pick something and put it on." Alice returned to her lipstick, and Giselle recommended that I wear the shiny, pink shirt, because it was so thin that it disappeared under the dance floor lights. Alice echoed Giselle's recommendation.

I realized that I was fighting a losing battle, so I located the bag and began rummaging through the items. Alice now worked on her eye makeup, and Giselle giggled at my surrender. I found five pieces of clothing: a red, form-fitting dress; a shiny, pink shirt; a white, spandex miniskirt; a neon orange thong; a black, fish-net shirt. Against my will, I pulled on the holey shirt. "You look fabulous, Jack. Simply fabulous!," Giselle squealed. "Now, come closer and let me apply some makeup to your cute, beaten face."

"Wait a minute; the shirt is as far as I'll go,

okay? No makeup, Giselle."

Giselle rolled her eyes, but she didn't argue the point. Instead, she quickly sprayed me twice with some perfume and said, "Elizabeth Taylor," and handed me the bottle of vodka. I took two swigs, coughed, and returned the bottle. She looked at me the same way some people look at a stray animal: pity wrapped in hope. She then lit a cigarette and gave it me. Empathy floated in her eyes. "Lets' go inside, honey. It's much cozier in there," she said with a broken smile.

CHAPTER 8

The three of us stepped out of the Ford Thunderbird and prepared to enter the nightclub. The streetlight's pale yellow light showered down on the ladies and exposed their physical attributes. Alice stood taller than Giselle and wore a brunette colored wig that draped beyond her broad shoulders and dangled to the middle of her back. The blunt lines on her face and her semi-squared jawline that rested heavily on her thick neck chased away plausibility of Alice being a true female. Quite honestly, between you and I, Alice looked like a college quarterback in pink, booty shorts, a nude-colored blouse, black bra, and a pair of red, strappy, high heels. But, it wasn't until she draped the white, feathered boa around her neck that she honestly became Alice. She transformed before my eyes. Much like Clark Kent tearing out of his business suit, Alice powered up, putting every ounce of femininity on display for all to notice. Her big hand swirled around her body, misting herself with perfume, making her sparkle with infused light. She appeared proud and liberated. I'd never seen anything like that in my life; I was bewildered. She reminded me of some kind of transsexual superhero, ready to dance to disco and pop pills and drink until her knight in shiny pleather takes her home. My attention shifted to a giggling Giselle, as she smoothed out any wrinkle from her fishnet stockings.

Unlike Alice, Giselle possessed a smaller build with shoulder-length, blond hair. Two, red, sparkling barrettes held back several stands of bangs, giving way to her androgynous facial structure. Her denim miniskirt and red, spandex shirt hugged her torso well and left nothing to the imagination. And her breasts, they appeared to be natural, not like Alice's surgically implanted job, which left me a little puzzled. A gust of wind swept through the street and sent a chill up my spine, and I noticed a cat walk out of the shadows and cross the street with a relaxed gait, as though she had crossed this street a thousand times.

I remained silent and smoked my cigarette, pretending not to notice Alice and Giselle adjusting their private parts. When I looked down the street again, the cat was gone, as if she never was there, but she was, if only for a moment.

"Okay, that should do it. Are you ready, Alice?," Giselle asked, plucking my smoke from my hand, taking a drag, and flicking it away.

"Yeah. I hate these damn fingernails," Alice said, walking away from the car.

I followed a pace behind them, drifting in a stream of French perfume, as they click-clacked their way to the club. I turned back to memorize where the car was parked, but realized I had forgotten its color.

The muscular and thick-mustached doorman greeted Alice and Giselle with hugs and kisses. He then proceeded to undress me with his eyes and gave Alice and Giselle a look of approval. "Well, hello, there, chipmunk," he said, with a big, inviting smile. He eyed me long and hard, mentally entertaining himself for a moment. Alice and Giselle chuckled at the doorman's flirtation and pushed me into the club.

Disco dance hits played behind the red, velvet curtain. The mid-sized room was warm and dark and smelled of hard alcohol and women's fragrances. Up front, under a truss of colored lights, a short stage and runway protruded into the audience. Giselle located a booth near the back of the place, so we made it ours. The bouquet of colored lights shined on a Demi Moore look-a-like, as she lip-synched Madonna's *Like A Virgin*. There was no question that she had watched countless hours of

Madonna videos, because she had all the moves, all the poses, all the expressions. She was Madonna reincarnate, except with a tucked-away penis.

Her performance rendered an emphatic round of applause and catcalls. Some audience members enjoyed the act so much that they tossed money on the stage. As the Demi Moore look-a-like disappeared behind a tinsel curtain, another entertainer took the stage. I sat in silence and watched the spectacles, one right after another. Alice scanned the room looking for Xavier. She became excited when she spotted him standing at the bar and excused herself and made her way across the room.

As the performances continued, Giselle and I sat in the booth with silence between us. She acknowledged a few people who waved at her and immediately slid out of the booth when an older man wearing a sea captain's hat waved her over. She straightened her miniskirt and added an exaggerated sway to her hips as she approached him. She hugged and kissed him on both cheeks, and they exchanged a few words and disappeared out of sight.

"This is fucking fantastic!," I thought. I'm sitting alone in a room filled with flamboyant, lip-syncing trannies, trying to blend into the background and avoid eye contact with strangers, as I wait and hope for Giselle's prancing return. I scanned the room and found Alice mingling with the casual-comfort of a regular, and it appeared as Xavier really had something for Alice. He rested his arm around her waist and whispered into her ear, which made her throw her head back and chuckle and squeeze his ass. The two seemed to go together like a hot dog in a bun. I shifted my sights back to the stage and wondered why Crumbs and Charlie left without me. Cursing those sons of bitches, I tried figuring out how I could reconnect with those two assholes.

Alice, Giselle, and Xavier talked to each other at the bar. They laughed and carried on as good friends do before Giselle excused herself and headed back in my direction. She had a small, drink tray in hand, and smiled when I came in to view. "See, I told you," she said, as she sat down with a raised eyebrow. "I always get things done, honey. One way or another." She lowered her sights to the items on the tray and giggled at her procurement. The tray held two joints; two glasses of water; several vicodin pills; and a small first-aid kit. I was completely impressed.

"Where did you find this stuff?"

"From Captain, silly."

"You mean, the old, fat dude with the hat?"

"Yes, but don't let him hear you say that, Jack. He's one of the nicest men you'll ever meet. Now, sit still while I clean you up. It's going to sting a little bit, okay?"

"If it must," I said, offering Giselle my beaten face.

Giselle opened the kit and began her Florence Nightingale work; she cleaned my wounds with an antiseptic wipe, filled the cuts with Neosporin, and sealed them shut with Band-Aids.

"See, all brand new. You know, it kind of makes you look tough and sexy, too," she said, and closed the first-aid kit.

"That's good. I need to remember that the next time I'm getting the shit kicked out of me."

"Ah, don't be like that, Jacky. No pouting over the past. There's nothing we can do to change it. Besides, we're here to have fun. Fun, remember? So, let's have it; pass me my purse, sweetness."

Giselle produced the bottle of vodka from her shiny purse, took a hearty swig, and chased it with water, then handed me the bottle. As I tilted the bottle, Giselle put a pill on the tip of her tongue and made it disappear. She placed a pill in front of me and watched on. I followed her lead without missing a beat, which made her smile.

"You're such a good boy, Jack. I'm going to have to keep an eye on you," she said. "I'm wise to your kind."

Moments later, Captain strolled over to our

booth and introduced himself to me and didn't hesitate to mention that Giselle deserves a good man in her life, one who will treat her like a lady, with class and sophistication. I agreed; what else could I have said?

"Giselle, here, told me that you put yourself in harm's way to defend her lifestyle, our lifestyle, is that right, Jack? Is this true?," he asked, rubbing his white chin whiskers while staring at me with the seriousness of an overly-protective father.

"Uh, defending... yes, of course, defending. Always in harm's way, defending the lifestyle, I mean, come on, look at me, look at my face, what else was I supposed to do?," I said, glancing at a giggling Giselle, then back at a now proud and grinning Captain.

"Yes, indeed. That's very good. Very good, my boy, very good piece of news around here, as you may know, not many men would do what you did, Jack. Not many. Sure, they say they would, but when it comes down to it, they would run away scared. I know it. They know it. They're cowards. You understand? Let me tell you something, okay? Is that okay, Jack?," he asked, stepping closer and leveling his eyes with mine.

"Please, tell me anything you'd like, anything," I said, smelling the booze on his hot breath.

"I wish I could say this more often, but I can't, and it's unfortunate, but what can I do? But, tonight is different— because, tonight, I can, so I'm going to tell you— Jack, my boy, you have really big balls, and I respect that about you. Sure, you always hear about a big dick, everybody has. It's nothing new and that's fine. But, let me tell you, it's not about having a big dick, Jack."

"It isn't?," I asked, shifting my eyes to Giselle, then back to a serious Captain, "Because, I thought that every—"

"Sure. But, that's for people who always go after the low hanging fruit in life. It's easy and simple. A, b, c, 1, 2, 3. Where are the brains in that? But, let me ask you something, what's a dick without balls? Huh, what is it?"

Captain's question left me speechless for a moment; my mind was bewildered, because I never thought about it. I stammered for an answer, other than the obvious, before he kindly interrupted.

"Don't worry about it; you and Giselle have fun tonight. It'll all make sense to you in time, because, if I learned anything in all my years, it's not about the size of one's dick that counts, not in the real world; it's about the size of one's balls. And, you either have then, or you don't. That's it. No other way about it. Anyway, I admire your bravery. You sound like a good guy to me," Captain said, straightened his posture and tapped my shoulder. "Hey, listen, whenever you come to my place, you tell the doorman, Pump, that you want to see Captain, and I'll make sure that you get taken care of. We're friends now, understand? Don't be a stranger."

"Of course, and thank you," I said.

"By the way, nice nipples, kid," he said, then gestured to a waitress to bring us drinks and walked away.

I remained surprised and speechless.

"See, you're on Captain's good side, just like that," she said, picking up the two joints from the tray. "I feel like getting high, don't you?"

"Yeah, but, what about our drinks?"

"They'll be waiting for us when we get back. Follow me," she said, sliding out of the booth and into the crowd.

I followed a step behind her, realizing we had to cut through the small dance floor to get to the backyard area; and when the dance crowd grew thick, Giselle reached back, found my hand, and took a hold of it, leading us deeper onto the dance floor. I shouted her name and tried letting go of her hand, but she only held on tighter. And before I knew it, we were surrounded by fabulous people, all dancing, all having fun, as though the night would go on forever. I couldn't say which song was playing at that moment, not for certain, but I think it was Culture Club's *Do You Really*

Want To Hurt Me? The music was loud, and the mirror ball that rotated above us sprinkled tiny dots of white light upon the walls. Giselle swayed her hips and said, "Come on, Jack. Dance with me. Dance with me. It's just a dance," then placed her hand on my shoulder and got lost in the moment. And, she was right.

When the song blended into the next, she became excited, as one does when hearing her favorite song. And, I knew she wasn't going to let me off the dance floor until the song ended, but I had to try, nonetheless. "Oh, my God, I love this song," she shouted, stepped in closer and began shimming about. As she rocked her body to the beat, the dance floor lights shined upon her red, rhinestone barrettes and made them sparkle with glimmering flashes of light, and the thought I had of leaving the dance floor disappeared from my mind.

I must be honest, I never danced with a woman like Giselle, but there we were, dancing under a blend of colorful lights, and she appeared happy and carefree, and there was something very special about that. Every now and again, she would look at me with her heavy-mascara eyes and sing the words of that song, as though she has sung them a million times over. When I'd break eye contact, she would tug my shirt and again capture my attention. I believe she found humor in it; because each time she would get me to look back at her, she'd smile the kind of smile that teeters on joyful laughter and, knowing that feeling, made me smile until we were both laughing in the middle of a crowd of dancing strangers.

When Giselle grew tired of dancing, she led off us off the dance floor, headed toward the bar and ordered us a couple of vodka cocktails.

"I didn't know you were such a good dancer, Jack," she said, taking a sip of her drink. "Or, a gentleman, for that matter. Thanks for showing me a good time."

"Yeah, neither did I," I confessed, biting down on a piece of ice.

"Which one? Not knowing you were such a good dancer or being a gentleman?," she asked, now fanning herself with her hand. "Worked up a bit of perspiration, didn't we?"

"Both, I guess."

She smiled into her drink, paused a moment, then found my eyes and said, "Well, you don't always have to be a perfect gentlemen around me, Jack." She held her gaze long enough for me to realize her innuendo. When she finished her drink, she said, "Let's get us some fresh air, honey. What do you say?," then turned and walked back into the crowd.

The backdoor exited into a narrow but long patio area. There were 10 to 12 people standing around smoking, mingling, and making out.

Giselle sat down on the farthest bench from the crowd and lit the joint. City sounds mixed with the muffled dance beats. She took a few hits, passed me the joint, and looked away, exhaling, like a weightless person floating in between heaven and earth, detached without a care in the world. I watched and wondered about her life and how she came to be.

As we smoked, Giselle talked about San Francisco, about this and that, and how randomly cool it was to bump into me, even though the situation was unfortunate.

"It's so weird how life, the universe, God, whatever you want to call it, works, you know? Just think about it, I bet we would have never met in a million years and be hanging out together. It's kind of a trip, because we are, right now, right here, me and you, Jack, hanging out. Don't you find that a bit strange or amazing?"

"Actually, it's really—"

"Okay, like imagine for a minute, if when you woke up this morning, someone told you, 'Jack, later tonight, you'll be abandoned by your friends, mugged by a guy named, what was his name again?"

"Teddy."

"Right. 'Mugged by a guy named Teddy, rescued by two, fabulous-looking trannies, thank you very much, and end up in a transgender bar smoking a joint with an awesome person named Giselle?' I mean, what would you say? Fucking unreal, right?"

Her question left me dumbstruck.

"See, exactly, I just mind fucked you. You don't even know what to say, Jack, but here we are, right?," she said, taking a hit from the joint and passing it.

"Yes, this is true; here we are, and it's all still happening. You know, what?"

"What?"

"I'm so fucking high right now," I said, chuckling and handing over the joint.

"You fucking lightweight. Yeah, me, too," she said, taking another hit. "Let's go find more drinks. Come on."

I blurred my way back inside the club and reappeared in our booth, sitting with a drink in my hand. Alice and Xavier were both sitting in the booth snorting small piles of white powder off the back of Xavier's hand, talking and laughing, and carrying on like two, modern day romantics. Giselle nudged Xavier in his ribs and made her eyebrows jump up and down. He then offered us a sampling of his goods; however, I declined his offer.

"Hey, *amigo*, let me say this to you. This crank is so fucking good; it will make your scratches, the ones on your face, heal up so fast and so fucking good. The sun, you know, the sun, up there, it won't even have a chance to shine on them. For real, man. You take this one, okay, my friend," he said, shoving the top of his fist under my nose.

I inhaled the small pile of white powder and felt it burn the back of my throat.

"Here, take a drink," Alice insisted, pushing a glass into my hand. "Yeah, boy, you know it's like fire. Drink up and wash it down."

The three of them discussed trivial topics until *It's Raining Men* began playing. Alice grabbed Xavier's hand and pulled him onto the dance floor. Giselle pulled a compact mirror from her purse and inspected her nose for powder rings.

"How are you feeling, sweet cheeks?"

"Better. When does this place close?"

"Oh, I'd say, in an hour or so. When I get really trashed, Captain lets me sleep it off in the storage room. It's through that door, right there, down those stairs. He's got an old couch in there; it's kind of dirty, though. Or, if you want—," she said, closed her compact and tossed it in her purse. "You could crash at my place. It's nothing special, but it's home, and I could cook us some food. You could take a shower and call your friends or whatever. It's your choice. I don't live far from here, but it's completely up to you. It's just another option, you know?"

I didn't know what to do or say, so I said the first thing that entered my mind, "Where's the restroom?"

Giselle exhaled and answered, "I'll show you, follow me; it's in the back, honey, in the corner; it's unisex, isn't that funny? I mean— oh, never mind. Come on."

In the restroom, Giselle went to the mirror, and I entered a stall. On the floor, right side of the toilet, I saw evidence that someone believed in littering and practicing safe sex. I tried urinating, but couldn't. I wasn't sure if it was Giselle's talking, the sight of the dirty condom, or the slurping and moaning sounds coming from the next stall, so I zipped up and walked out of the restroom.

When we returned to our booth, Alice and Xavier were going at it again, like two teenagers. He stopped kissing Alice and proposed that we all go back to his place to party. Alice agreed. Xavier added that we could leave Alice's car at the club, and we could all ride with him. Again, Alice agreed. A snap decision was upon me: go to Xavier's; sleep on Captain's dirty couch in the storage room; or, go to Giselle's. It was obvious: Giselle was the safest bet.

Alice and Giselle, like most women,

huddled up to have a private discussion before the officially plan was decided, and they decided that Alice and Xavier would go their way, and Giselle and I would go our way. And with that being said, the four of us made our way out of the booth, toward the club's exit, and out onto the street.

The wind pushed the fog through the city's damp streets, and we all shivered as Alice rifled about in her purse. She found her keys, handed them to Giselle, and said, "Please drive slow and please, please, please, keep it in between the white lines this time, Giselle."

"Yes, ma'am, no swerving this time," she said, with an exaggerated salute.

"I'm serious, Giselle. Please be careful."

"I know," she said, slouching her shoulders.

Alice delivered a piecing stare of concern and spurred Giselle to repeat herself.

"I said, I know. Now, get out of here and take your boyfriend with you. And, you mister, you better treat her like a lady tonight."

Giselle playfully closed one eye and shook her finger at Xavier.

"No, I will not. I will not treat her like a lady. I— I will treat her like— a woman," Xavier confessed, and then skirted Alice away toward his car. "A woman, I tell you!"

The sound of Alice's click-clacking heels and Xavier's drunken laughter dissipated into the night.

CHAPTER 9

Giselle and I walked a half block back to Alice's car, shivering our asses off the entire way. After jumping in the car and starting its engine, we sat frozen against the chilled, vinyl seats, like two stiffs waiting to be driven to the morgue. Our teeth rattled, as we tried warming our hands with our white breath, but that didn't work, so Giselle turned on the heater, but the damn thing only blew cold air on us. Giselle cursed the heater and revved the engine, until we felt the cold air begin to warm the interior and defrost the windshield.

She gripped the transmission handle and shifted it to drive, looked at me, then my frozen nipples and said, "Damn, those things look hard enough to cut diamonds. Is your jacket still in the back? Take a look." As I turned and leaned into the backseat, Giselle punched the gas pedal and sent me flying into the backseat. All I heard was her giggling and the car's powerful V8 engine growling, as we sped off into the dark. On my back, stretched out across the backseat, my thoughts crashed into each other and, although, I wanted to ask Giselle where she lived, the only words that found their way out of my mouth at that moment were, "Turn on the radio, the radio, okay?" Giselle mumbled something and laughed and then music was heard. I can't remember the name of the song, but it sounded familiar, and I think it was The Cure. I soon closed my eyes to a string of blurred streetlights and concentrated on my breathing; it was slow and heavy, and I felt my body relax and my thoughts slip into the primordial unconsciousness.

"Hey, Jack, I can't carry you. Jack... wake up... Jack?," a loud voice said. My eyes opened to Giselle yanking my arm and telling me to wake the hell up. "We're here," she said. "Wake up, Jack. We're home." I climbed out of the backseat and followed Giselle up the street, up a stairway, and into a warm apartment. She talked and I tried listening to the words, but her red, sparkling barrettes were distracting, so I smiled and gravitated toward the couch. She disappeared into her bedroom and began listening to her answering machine. She skipped through most of the messages and returned with a pillow and a red and black colored blanket. The place smelled of vanilla and stale smoke. "I need to eat something; I'm starved," she said, walking toward the kitchen. "You want leftover pizza? Good. Because, that's all I got."

We ate in silence, more or less; and when we were done eating, Giselle turned on her small television and closed the window blinds. She offered a hot shower and a joint. Although, I must admit, at the time, a hot shower would've been perfect, but I awkwardly declined, and we smoked the joint instead. After a few hits, she stood and said, "Help yourself to whatever you want, Jack. There's water in the fridge. I need a shower before bed, so goodnight, sweetheart." Giselle turned off the T.V. and disappeared out of the semi-dark living room, leaving me on her couch under a soft, warm blanket. As I sailed off to sleep, I heard Giselle walk down the hall and close the bathroom door. Soon, the sound of falling water filled her apartment, and I thankfully drowned in it.

The smell of toast, bacon, and fresh brewed coffee was my wake up call. As I opened my eyes and took in the unfamiliar view, I couldn't help but panic at first. All was quiet, and it felt like a twisted and dreamy hangover. "Where the fuck am I?," I thought, while sprawled out on a stranger's couch. I tried piecing together the previous night's events, but I couldn't, because I was still too drunk. My body ached in random places and my head pounded, as if it didn't care that it belonged to me. From the kitchen, a soft voice asked, "Would you like some coffee, sunshine?" I attempted to answer and began coughing. The urge to urinate commanded me off the couch and toward the bathroom.

I entered the bathroom, closed the door, and used my foot to lift the toilet seat. While aiming into the toilet, the room spun and I thought I was going to fall, so I reached out my hand. I peed on the toilet paper roll and the floor and almost yanked a towel rack off the wall, but I did not fall. As I stood still, regaining my balance, I noticed something that sent my thoughts reeling out of control. The buttons of my fly were already unbuttoned when I stepped to the toilet. But, wait… did I unbutton them? Did I forget to button them sometime last night? Did I unbutton them in my sleep? I didn't know how, who, or why my pants were unbuttoned, but I did know that they were unbuttoned. Panic and confusion unloaded on me like machine guns, shooting me full of holes. "What exactly happened last night?," I asked under my breath.

"Are you okay in there? There's more toilet paper under the sink if you need it, okay?," she asked, through the door.

"Okay. Hey, um, I—"

"Yeah."

"Never mind. It's fine."

"Is everything alright, Jack?"

"Yes, everything's fine. I'll be out in a

minute."

"Well, there's breakfast on the table, and your coffee's getting cold."

Questions swirled in my mind like booze in a nameless cocktail. I removed the Band-Aids and washed my face and brushed my teeth with my finger and a glob of toothpaste. As I washed my hands, I must confess, the mirror held a sad sight, definitely one of the worst sights of myself to date. I figured all of last night's details would return to me later, one by one; then, I remembered meeting Giselle and Alice and Teddy and drinking with Crumbs and Charlie and… it all became too much to try to decipher at the moment, so I toweled my hands and opened the door to a new day.

Giselle had draped a lavender-colored kimono over her small-framed body and had eye shadow and nail polish to match. She sort of reminded me of a geisha, a San Francisco kind of geisha, perhaps, but without the black hair and white face makeup. She sat behind a plate of food and sipped her coffee with the grace of a resting butterfly.

"How did you sleep? Pretty good, I imagine. You were passed out cold this morning, like a sack of rocks, dead to the world. There's cream and sugar on the counter, if you want it. So, how do you feel, should I ask?"

"Worse than I look, I guess," I said, sitting down to breakfast.

"Yeah, your scratches don't look too bad, but we'll clean them again anyway," she said, sipping her coffee.

I chewed on toasted bread and washed it down with coffee and looked at Giselle over the rim of my cup, much like a stray dog looks up from his bowl, food in its mouth and gratitude in its eyes. "What happened last night? I can remember some stuff, but, to tell you the truth, not most of it," I admitted, taking a bite of bacon.

Giselle told me of Teddy and how he mugged me in an alley and how she and Alice saved me and how we partied at the club and talked about life and smoked joints and drank cocktails under the stars. "I must've blacked out on the drive home," she said with a hint of embarrassment. "Because, I don't remember a thing, totally on autopilot, like a spaced-out robot. Blacked out, blacked out, blacked out, oh, look, I'm home. Hello? It's kind of like teleportation or something. Sorry. I'm still in work in progress, I suppose."

When we finished eating, Giselle asked if I had any thoughts on finding Crumbs and Charlie. She plucked a joint from the ashtray, lit it, and waited for my answer, which never came. I returned to the couch and stared listlessly at the television screen. A silent sadness sat between us, as a white, morning blanket of fog lingered outside the kitchen window. Giselle shifted in her seat, angled her back toward me, and smoked the joint while gazing outside. "It looks like it's going to rain soon... or, maybe, not. Maybe, it's just me," she mumbled. Her words disappeared into a cloud of smoke. For the first time since meeting Giselle, she appeared sad and alone. I watched her breathe through a private, intimate moment in her life, as if she was the only person in the room. At that moment, she was, and I was nothing more than a passing spectator to a disappearing watercolor painting of a geisha sitting at a window.

Minutes later, when she noticed that the joint had gone out, she tossed it back into the ashtray and began clearing the table. She hummed a little tune that brought a tiny smile to her face. And, when she had finished, she advised that I dial the telephone operator and ask for Charlie's phone number, which I did; however, after several unsuccessful attempts, I discovered that Charlie Steelman had a non-published phone number, but I wasn't surprised. I returned the phone receiver to its cradle and rubbed my tired eyes.

I had two strikes on me: I didn't have Charlie's new phone number or his new address. Giselle's idea of driving me back to Charlie's apartment was useless. However, she offered to drive to where she found me, the piss-stinking alley.

"There's a bar next to the alley, maybe, we should start there," she said, with a press-on smile.

"There is? That makes sense."

"What does?"

"It stunk like piss in there, like a fucking urinal. I bet people leave the bar and piss in there all the time. I know I would. It makes sense. Do you know the name of the bar?"

"Sorry, honey. I don't. But, maybe, the bartender knows Charlie. It is a neighborhood bar, right? Hey, maybe, that Teddy guy walked you in circles. You never know. He could've, right? I don't know. It's possible. At least say it's possible, so I don't feel stupid, okay?"

"Yeah, it's possible, anything's possible, but, man, that's a stretch."

"Listen, I know it's not much to go on. It's a long shot. I realize that, but it's the only shot you got."

What could I say? She was right, and she knew the exact spot of where she found me, so she already knew more than me on the subject. What could I say?

"Do you have a better idea, Jack?"

"No, but I wish I did."

"It's not much, but, it gives us an excuse to get a drink, right? Fuck it. What do you got to lose?"

"Yeah— fuck it. Let's go."

I felt optimistic about reconnecting with Crumbs and Charlie. Giselle offered me a shower again, and again, I declined. She giggled, as if she knew something I didn't and disappeared into the bedroom to change out of her kimono. She reappeared wearing tight jeans, a baggy, purple sweatshirt, and large-lensed sunglasses. She snatched the car keys off the counter and said, "After you, sweet cheeks." She followed me out of her apartment and down to the street.

Daylight punched me in the eyes and kicked me in the head. I felt nauseous and clammy under my clothes, but there was nowhere to hide. I imagined I felt like one of those desperate and unfortunate vampires playing on the big screen, retreating from the sun with his skin ablaze, moments from exploding. I watched Giselle unlock the driver side door and step inside and lean over and unlock the passenger door. Inside the car, I watched her insert the key into the ignition and start the car and pump the gas pedal several times to warm the engine. "Why are you moving so slow? It's like you're in slow motion. Can't you see I'm a vampire and about to explode in Alice's car? Let's get these wheels moving, sister, like now," I thought.

Giselle gripped the transmission shift knob and dropped it into drive and drove away from the curb, and I exhaled with relief.

"Is everything okay? You're looking really pale, Jack."

"Can I borrow your sunglasses? My head hurts."

"No, they're woman sunglasses. I mean, of course, I'd let you borrow them, but I need them. Look in the glove box. Can you light me a ciggy? They're in my purse."

Her request confused me. I didn't know what to do first, get Giselle a smoke or look for a pair of sunglasses. I squinted and filled her request. The cigarette smoke churned my stomach and my mouth began to water and I knew I was about to get sick. While Giselle was talking and puffing on her cigarette, I leaned out the window and released projectile vomit onto the misfortunate cars parked along the street.

"Shit, Jack, that was fucking disgusting," she said, with true amusement. "Oh, my God, dude, that was really gross, okay."

She laughed, flicked her cigarette out of the car, and turned on the radio.

"Sorry, but I had to. I had no choice."

"That's for sure. I'd hate to see that the day after Thanksgiving. Do you feel better?

Ready for a beer?"

"Yes and yes. I do feel better."

"Good."

Giselle drove onward, making several left and right turns, and talked about this and that and the other. She said that I should consider myself lucky for not being stabbed and not to worry about the stolen money, because money comes and goes, and it will always be that way for people like us, and it's better that we come to terms with that fact sooner than later. While she continued, I wondered how my pants became unbuttoned and why Crumbs and Charlie left me.

"Thank your lucky stars that you're here with only a few scratches. They make me so mad, those good-for-nothing punks. They think they own the streets. I can't stand it. Hey, does this street look familiar, honey?," she asked. "It's up there on the left side. You see it? That's where we found you last night, Jack."

I did see the alley, but it was no different that any other alley I've seen before. There wasn't anything familiar or recognizable about it. It was a dirty alley on the side of some bar. Nothing more; not to mention, it was really dark last night and I was shamefully drunk. Giselle found a parking space a block away from the bar and told me to lock my door, as she stepped out onto the street.

As I approached the alley, a strange feeling swept over me, a sort of displaced sense of being, as if being physically and emotionally lost for a moment. I stopped at the alley's mouth and looked inside, and it welcomed us with its pungent odor of urine. I saw myself talking to Teddy and remembered his watery, jaundice-colored eyes and the sound of his footsteps trailing off into the dark.

"Should we check to see if anything was left behind?" Giselle asked, but what echoed in my ears was Teddy saying, "Go down motherfucker; you're beat. Stupid-ass-motherfucker!"

"If anything was, I'm sure it's no longer there. Fuck it, let's get a beer," I said, turning away from the alley.

Giselle ordered us a couple of drafts, and I scanned the bar, hoping to remember something, anything, but nothing came to mind, other than the huge jukebox. Then, I recalled Crumbs and Charlie talking to those two ladies, who were sitting at the end of the bar. "Those bastards sold me out for pussy. No, they didn't; they wouldn't; there had to be something more than just the pusskits and gravy," I thought.

When the bartender brought us another round, I asked him if he knew Charlie, which puzzled him for a minute, because he instantly froze up and his eyes rolled around his head, as if his brain was about to short circuit.

"Charlie… Charlie… Charlie… Charlie, right? Let me think. How does he look?"

"Well, he's about this tall, but he's really not tall, not really; he's shorter than me, so he's kind of short, but don't tell him that, because he doesn't like to hear it, and he has short, brown, blond hair, and he's—"

"Oh, wait a minute… Charlie… has short, brown hair, and he's shorter than you… Charlie. Let me think. Give me a minute. Stand up. Anything else?"

"He's always smiling, sort of like this."

"Oh, do that again, but push your upper lip higher and pick up your beer and look right at me."

"You mean, like this?"

"Higher, so your upper lip tucks way above your teeth."

"Like this?"

"Higher."

"It can't go any higher. Shit."

"Wait a minute… keep looking at me… look right at me… hold it… just like that… wait a minute… Charlie, right?"

"Yes."

"I think I do know him; I mean, we're not friends, but yeah, I know that guy, kind of. He sold me a deep-sea fishing pole, pretty damn good one and cheap, too. I used that thing a few weeks ago, up in Seattle. He's got capped teeth, the front ones, maybe, too big for his mouth. What about him?"

Giselle smiled and raised her eyebrows; and in between gulps of beer, I explained how Charlie and Crumbs ditched me last night. He laughed, as he rummaged through his wallet, pulled out a stack of frayed business cards, and handed them to me.

"I think his number might be on the back on one of those cards," he said, walking away toward another customer. I dealt the business cards onto the counter with the precision of a Las Vegas card dealer. Giselle and I eyed the back of each card and found nothing. Then, she flipped over the closest card to her, giggled, and held it before my eyes. The card read: Charlie. Deep-sea fishing pole. Call him. Charlie's phone number was scribbled underneath the note.

She handed me the business card and took a long drink from her glass. "Any luck, the bartender asked, walking toward us. I held up the card, and he pointed to the pay phone. Giselle laid some change on the bar with a smile. I scooped up the quarters and walked to the make the call.

In all honesty, I didn't imagine Giselle's plan actually working. That's not to say, that her plan didn't make sense. Her plan made complete sense, but just because something makes sense doesn't mean it's going to work. Everybody knows that, right? Retrace your steps and begin. Sometimes, long shots pay off; and when they do, they pay big.

I dropped the coins into the phone and pushed in his number. And just like that, I heard Charlie say, "Hello?"

"You fucking asshole."

"Jack? Jack, buddy, where in the hell are you?"

"Where am I? Are you shitting me?"

Charlie's roaring laughter filled my ear.

"I'm where you left me?"

"What? You're still at the Gold Digger?"

"Yeah, man, whatever it's called. At the bar."

More painful laughter entered my ear.

"Don't go anywhere, Jack. I'm on my way."

I hung up the phone and an overwhelming feeling of completion washed over me. Help was on the way.

When I returned to my seat, Giselle and the bartender offered ways of getting back at Charlie. One proposed act of revenge was to shave off one of Charlie's eyebrows while he slept, another was to flood his bathroom by flushing a potato and unbolting his toilet from the floor. They offered more ideas, and we shared a few more laughs before the bartender left us to our beers.

Giselle grew silent and finished her beer. We knew we'd soon be parting ways, and the awkward energy between us proved it. I must admit, I teetered between joy and sadness about returning to our own private, personal lives. I was joyful for the obvious reasons and saddened for the not so obvious. I mean, after being beaten, robbed, and stranded in some alley to rot, I met complete strangers who willingly stepped into my situation. Unfortunately, most of us know, that most people wouldn't jump into a sinking ship to save someone, especially a drunk and bleeding stranger. But, Alice and Giselle did. They picked me up, dusted me off, and Giselle stayed with me until I found my way again.

At that moment, I was heavyhearted, because she and I knew we would never meet again. Sure, we said we would continue our budding friendship; who wouldn't? It's the appropriate thing to say; it's even somewhat expected, but the truth supersedes all. But the truth was, our worlds would never collide again, at least, not in this lifetime.

"So, Charlie's coming to get you, huh? I bet you can't wait to take a shower and sleep in your own bed, am I right?"

"Yeah."

"Yeah. I know the feeling. Sometimes, we take the most basic things in our lives for granted. It's strange, isn't it?

I looked at Giselle, at her friendly eyes behind her cool, large-lensed sunglasses, and grinned.

"What?," she asked. Her question hanged vulnerably off her crooked, little smile.

"Thank you for everything. I mean it."

"Ah, ain't you the sweetest of the bunch, Jack."

She scribbled something on a cocktail napkin and placed it in my hand.

"Here's my number. You do anything you wish with it, okay? But, I hope you keep it and call me sometime. And, don't take this as a come on, sweetie. It's simply a way to contact me… for the next time you find yourself in the city, okay? Now, come here, so I can give you a hug, if you don't mind."

As I hugged her, Giselle whispered, "Take care of yourself, honey," and then walked out of the bar. I saved her number and waited for Charlie to arrive.

There's an uncomfortable feeling one gets when sitting at a bar without any money, behind an empty glass, and having nowhere to go. I sipped the remaining suds slowly. The bartender eyed me a couple of times, as if asking, "You ready for another?" I nodded no and looked down at my empty glass, but he read my situation better than I guessed, because he brought me a fresh beer and said, "It's on me, man. No worries, Chief."

Some fifteen minutes passed before Charlie entered the bar. Without saying a word, he sat down next to me, gripped the nape of my neck, and said, "Jesus, son, you had your mother and I worried sick. You didn't call. We thought you were dead in some ditch somewhere. Don't ever do that again." Then, he laughed and hugged me so hard I nearly fell off my barstool.

"That's real fucking funny, Charlie. Where's Crumbs?"

"Crumbs?"

"Yeah, Crumbs. Where is he?"

The bartender placed two beers in front of us.

"He went home this morning."

"He, what?"

"Relax. I'll give you a ride. Man, look at your face. Oh, come on, Jack, don't look at me like that. It wasn't my fault. You got to believe me, man. Really, it wasn't. We got caught up in the middle of some bullshit, and I'm going to tell you all about it, but not here, not now," he said, taking a gulp of beer. "Things kind of got screwed up, which I had no control over, and I was totally wasted, too, which didn't help any. So, you're just going to have to believe me on this. By the way, who popped you in your face? Does this hurt?"

Charlie quickly pressed his thumb against the cut above my eyebrow and, when I grimaced, he chuckled and said, "Now, you have something to whine about. But, don't worry, because today is a new day. Now, drink your beer, son. I have plans for us."

CHAPTER 10

When we finished our beers, we drove to a nearby diner called Uncle Bunker's Café on 9th Avenue. We sat in a threadbare booth near the back of the place, near the restroom, and the entire time we ate, Charlie wouldn't shut up about how much he loved pancakes, especially after a night of drinking. He swore pancakes were the best food after a belly full of booze. And, although he sounded like a man who had never eaten pancakes before, I couldn't argue with him. I mean, who argues with a person who buys you a stack of warm, buttermilk pancakes?

After we licked our plates clean, we sat in the booth like two, fat, panda bears and drank coffee. I gave Charlie the run-down on what happened to me after he and Crumbs disappeared. He apologized a couple of times and I believed him and let it go. I didn't see the point in holding a grudge, so I sipped my coffee and listened to his side of the story.

"After we left the bar last night, we left with those two chicks, and we stood outside waiting for you, but you were taking a dump and—"

"Look, all I know is, is that we were having a good time drinking and bullshitting, and I left to take a piss; and when I came back, you and Crumbs were gone. Exit stage left, man, just like that. You guys were fucking gone. And get this, while I'm looking for you, this dude starts telling me his life story and lures me into an alley and jumps me…"

Charlie drank his coffee and rubbed his whiskers with concern.

"I'm real lucky Teddy didn't put me in the hospital, man. He could've stabbed my guts. Shit, at least, I can say that. Thank God, I didn't end up on a gurney in some overcrowded hospital last night, because, if I did, I wouldn't be here right now with a stomach full of fucking pancakes and coffee. I'll tell you that much. I'm lucky, Charlie, real fucking lucky."

"Yeah, well, if your ass ended up in jail last night, instead of making new friends, we would've all been together, maybe, even have shared the same cell. They would've gotten us all, the whole enchilada, so, I guess you really are fucking lucky."

"Are you serious? You guys spent the night in jail?"

"That's what I've been trying to tell you, but you wanted me to wait, so I held my tongue and waited."

Charlie took a sip of coffee and cleared his throat.

"You remember those two chicks, right?"

"Yeah, little tits and her fat friend."

"Right. Tits and Fatty. Well, while the four of us were waiting for you outside, they started talking about going somewhere else. They were cold and shivering, and you know how women get when they're cold, all fidgety and shit, so we walked them to their car, right? But, Fatty's car doesn't start; her battery's dead. So, Crumbs decides to be a hero and tells them to wait, like they're going anywhere. Where are they going? Nowhere. The fucking battery is dead. I don't know. Anyway, Crumbs runs to get his car, so he could jump Fatty's car. Good idea. Well, Tits decides we should all wait in Fatty's car, so we all climb into Fatty's car, me and Tits in the front and lonely Fatty in the back, right?"

"Where's Crumbs?"

"Crumbs drives up, double-parks, and sees us all in the car, and we're all making out in the front and I'm all over her, so he must've figured that—"

"Fuck that. I want to get some, too."

"Exactly, so Crumbs jumps in the backseat with Fatty, and everybody's wet and happy, right?"

"Yeah. Right."

"Wrong."

"Why?"

"Because, Fatty tells Crumbs to hook up the jumper cables first."

"Before she gives him—"

"So, like a good boy, Crumbs jumps to it."

"Because he wants—"

"Are you kidding me? Who doesn't? Anyway, he gets back in the car and I hear Fatty unbuckle his pants, and they're getting comfortable in the backseat. Now, this is where it gets kind of fucked up. Tits stops and, with my hand up her legs, asks 'How much is it worth to me?' I ignore her and keep going, but she asks again, so I'm like, 'What are you talking about? You're worth lots, baby,' and I go back to my business and unbutton my pants and—"

"Wait a minute. How much is she worth? What's that supposed to mean?"

"Aren't you listening? I know, I didn't get it at first either. That's why I ignored her, but I think she was asking for money. Well, she wasn't exactly trying to sell it outright, but she definitely wasn't going to give it away for free. She was really drunk; we all were, and she started acting weird about giving a blowjob in her friend's car in some alley to a stranger."

"To a stranger? What the hell?"

"I know, right? I told her, 'I'm not a stranger. I'm Charlie. Sure, we just met, but I'm not a stranger, not really. I'm Charlie.'"

"Sounds like a head trip."

"Yeah, no shit. But what makes it worse, Crumbs and Fatty are getting down in the backseat, likes it's nobody's business. And, Tits says, 'I'm not a sex addict, okay?' So, I agree and tell her I believe her."

"Oh, my God, dude."

"I'm not sure what do at this point. Do I offer her money? Do I ignore the whole 'What's it worth' comment? Surprisingly, though, no bullshit, I was hard the entire time, dude. I think it's because I drank whiskey shots. I don't know. Anyway, she pulls my pants down a little lower and says, 'I'm really not like this; I'm really not. That was before, but I think you're cool and I want to suck your dick, okay?'"

"Wholly shit. What did you say?"

"Okay."

"I don't see the problem."

"She's going down, and I have my eyes closed, and I hear a tapping on the window, so I open my eyes and see two cops shining their flashlights into the car, making Cyclops retreat into his sleeping bag. You know what I'm saying?"

"Yeah, go on."

"Anyway, they ran our names; we were double-parked, participating in lewd acts in public; Tits had a prior charge for solicitation and—"

"She was a prostitute?"

"Not last night, but, yeah, maybe, once or twice, and they found some weed in the ashtray, blah, blah, blah, impounded both cars; Crumbs had a stolen registration sticker and I mouthed off, and we spent the night in the holding tank. I think they let the chicks go, though. I don't know. Who cares? So, yeah, anyway, good times."

I sat speechless, as the middle-aged waitress approached and filled our cups. "Looks like you boys had your share of fun last night," she said with a smirk and walked away. Charlie smiled at his coffee, picked up the bill, and said, "Let's get out of this place. I'm bored."

"You ready to drive me home?"

"No, not just yet. I have a plan," Charlie confessed with a crooked smile.

CHAPTER 11

When we arrived at Charlie's apartment, Charlie discovered that a paycheck was waiting for him in his mailbox; and by the look on his face, I assumed the check amount was more than he had expected. He reached into a coin-filled, mason jar, which he kept in the kitchen, and pulled a handful of change. "There's a shirt and a pair of sweatpants in the bathroom, and the laundry detergent is under the sink. You can figure out the rest; I'm going to the bank, be back soon," he said and walked out the door.

Nature called me to the toilet, so I sat down and did my best impersonation of Rodin's *The Thinker*; and as I sat there, I felt a cold, hard, sensation digging into the left side of my pelvic area, near my hip. I scratched at it few times and pulled aside my shirt to get a look at the area. And, there it was: Giselle's red, sparkling barrette, caught in the mesh netting of Alice's shirt.

My eyes widened with surprise and, again, my mind became flooded with questions, but somehow, I couldn't believe the obvious. I tried my hardest to remember what exactly happened at Giselle's apartment, but my memories were as spotted as a pack of Dalmatians. And, in all honesty, at that moment, I couldn't distinguish reality from fantasy. How did her barrette find its way below my waistline? I was clueless.

I removed Giselle's sparkling barrette, wrapped it in toilet paper, and flushed the damn thing down the toilet, but the question remained. Even to this day, I wonder, if Giselle took the liberty of giving me oral sex, as I lay drunk in a dreamy conscious state on her couch. I will never know the answer to this question. Perhaps, it is best left unconfirmed.

Hours ago, Charlie asked where I had spent the night, and I said, "With a woman, in her apartment, but I can't tell you the address, because I don't know it. I was really wasted, and all the doors looked the same." He looked at me as if I was lying to him, and when he asked again, I told him the same answer, so he stopped asking. Truth be told, my answer wasn't a complete fabrication of the truth. I mean, I did spend the night in a woman's apartment, and her name was Giselle. Okay, okay, maybe, I did stretch the truth some, but not entirely. Technically, I only told half the truth, but most of us know that life isn't made up of absolutes, because if they were, most of us would be bored to death.

Allowing the shower water to warm, I held up the clothes Charlie left for me on the counter and knew they were too small. Charlie and his practical jokes, but I didn't care. I showered, toweled off, and dressed in the tight-fitting clothes. The sweatpants looked more like knickers and the sleeveless shirt was so damn thin and showed my mid drift that I knew Alice and Giselle would approve. I felt like a joke in these clothes, but they were clean and I had no other choice. I forced myself out of the apartment, through the complex, and into the laundry room.

When the laundry duties had finished, I felt grateful to slip back into warm, freshly washed clothes. My black jeans and tee shirt never seemed so comfortable. And to sweeten the moment, Charlie returned with a handful of groceries. We spend the next several hours eating bean and cheese burritos, drinking beer, and talking about life, our friends, and everything in between.

Charlie found a television program on basic fishing techniques. We watched two fishermen catch and release big mouth bass, and Charlie mumbled something about his stepfather and going fishing, and having fun on the bay, and then clammed up. I noticed that he had pulled the beer label clean off his bottle. Soon, Charlie started talking in a manner, as if I wasn't even in the room, but he obviously knew I was, because, every now and again, he would look right at me. It was sort of strange, and I believe that the two fishermen on the television program caused Charlie to recall memories of his childhood.

Charlie watched his hands work on another beer bottle label and confessed that he didn't really like his stepfather at first. He thought that Ramon was trying to take the place of his biological father and he hated the fact that Ramon was Mexican. Charlie admitted that he didn't even know what a Mexican was until his biological father told him, and he was also told that Mexicans should not be "involved" with white women, like his mother. Charlie appeared embarrassed of his confession, but realized that it was his biological father's boozing, cheating, and gambling ways that led to his parents' divorce, not Ramon.

Charlie continued, saying that it wasn't until one weekend, when his biological father failed to pick him up, that he became more open-minded to accepting Ramon as a friend. "Ramon taught me how to fish, how to work, and a bunch of other important shit that my father never did. He taught me the value of a dollar and of a man's word, and he never spoke badly of my mother or father, for that matter."

They spent many Saturdays boating on the San Francisco Bay together; on Charlie's 18th birthday, Charlie received the spare keys to Ramon's fishing boat. He told Charlie that he could use the boat whenever he wanted, but never to captain the boat drunk. Ramon made it clear that his boat is not to be used as a party boat and to never trust the sea, because the sea is more vicious than a wild beast. Charlie understood, and the boat keys still remain on Charlie's keychain.

When we finished the beers, Charlie and I left his apartment for Haight Street. We smoked a joint and searched for a parking space and eventually found one on Cole Street, near Waller Street. The scent of patchouli and marijuana swirled in the air and punched us in our noses. There was a dirty-clothed panhandler who held a cardboard sign that read, "Help a duck that's down on her luck and caught in the muck. How about a buck?" She pleaded that she needed a bus ticket home. I offered her a friendly smile, because that was all I could afford. Charlie dashed into a mini-market and returned with two packs of cigarettes and a candy bar; he gave me half and danced a little jig to the sound of a pair of steel drums. He appeared merry and stoned to the point of making me laugh aloud.

We walked by little bars, restaurants, and second-hand clothing stores, and everyone on the street had their own agenda. I noticed a couple having sex in a sleeping bag behind a row of bushes. They were young, dirty-faced and, most likely, runaways.

"Don't stare, man. You act like you've never seen people fucking before, Jack."

"It's not that."

"Then, what is it?"

"It's just that I've never seen people fucking in public."

Charlie laughed and almost tripped over a man sleeping on the sidewalk, then darted into a second-hand, clothing store, and I followed. He rifled through the racks of clothes, wandered over to the shelves of shoes, and blew over to the sales counter and struck up a flirty conversation with a sales girl. I lingered in the background and watched Charlie word up the cute, smiling creature. Charlie pointed to several sunglasses in the showcase and asked to see them. She placed pairs of sunglasses on the counter and pushed an oval-shaped mirror in front of Charlie's face. With each pair Charlie tried on, he posed for the sales girl and made silly faces, which made her smile and laugh. But in the end, Charlie didn't buy anything; he just got her phone number and left the store. I watched her watch Charlie walk

out to the street and knew the phone number she
gave him was true.

CHAPTER 12

Two blocks later, we found a pair of barstools and sat down on them. We were drinking again in some bar and everything seemed to be moving along nicely.   I left Charlie talking to the bartender and stepped outside for fresh air and a cigarette. Across the street, two women argued over something; real life entertainment unfolded before my eyes, and I stood in the front row and watched their drama.   As one of the women waved her arms around in protest, a tall, black-haired man unexpectedly touched my shoulder.

"Sorry, I didn't mean to scare you. I noticed you were smoking and thought that you might have an extra," he said, offering a quarter for a cigarette. He then tilted his head to one side in a robotic fashion and stared at the cut above my eyebrow, as I searched for my cigarettes. There was something odd about this man. I soon noticed that his pupils were extremely dilated, which gave his eyes the appearance of being completely black. His pale complexion clashed with the redness of his thin lips, as I handed him a cigarette.

"Keep your quarter; it's no problem."

"Thank you," he said and plucked the cigarette from my hand. "If you're not doing anything tonight, you should drop by the Mariposa Oscura."

He handed me a flyer to the nightclub, burned life into his cigarette, and said, "See, you tonight, friend," and walked away.

Moments later, Charlie stepped onto the street to smoke a smoke and found me reading the flyer.

"What do you got there, another coupon for a massage parlor? Does it say anything about a hot towel special? Because, I know of this little Korean place in the Tenderloin with the nicest chicks and for a hundred bucks, we could both get—"

"Easy, Ron Jeremy. It's a flyer for the Mariposa Oscura."

"Who's playing?"

"Fiendishly Dying."

"Yeah, you don't want to go there. Besides, you'll get the shit scared out of you.

Forget it."

"What do you mean? What is this place?"

Charlie looked away and pulled a long drag from his smoke, as if disinterested in the conversation.

"Trust me, crazy shit goes on there. I've seen it, man. We'd have a better time somewhere else. Take my word for it."

"Let's go check it out, unless you're scared or something. Are you scared, dude?"

Charlie looked at me for a moment, grinned devilishly, and pulled the last drag from his cigarette before flicking it out in to the street.

"I ain't scared. Hey, if you want to go to the Mariposa Oscura, who am I to try and stop you, you know? Fuck it, man. But, just remember, you asked for it, okay?"

"Sure. Whatever that's supposed to mean."

As Charlie and I returned to our barstools, he pulled me close and said, "I hope you brought your leather chaps with you, son."

We sat in those barstools until the sun disappeared, talking, drinking, talking, and drinking some more.

Before we walked out of that little bar, Charlie handed me a cocktail napkin with his new phone number scribbled on it, just in case. He also gifted me a five-minute phone card that he received for buying more than eight gallons of gas at his local gas station, which he and I found hilariously funny. I mean, what kind of conversation can anyone have in five minutes? I accepted the calling card, tucked it my back pocket, and returned to the street.

CHAPTER 13

The street took on a different persona than some hours ago: there were more cars, trucks, and bicycles, more people walking about, more chatter and laughter on the street. Artificial light and shadows freckled the sidewalks, and everyone carried on, as if they couldn't care less.

Charlie had a sway in his stride and wondered if he was too drunk to drive. We agreed that we needed another drink to decide, and after three pints, we decided that he wasn't too drunk to drive.

"Dude, I'm not that drunk; yeah, maybe, I am by police standards, but I'm really not; besides, the Mariposa isn't that far. Light me up a smoke, and let's go. I'm fine, believe me, okay?," Charlie said, pissing behind a bush.

I knew he was lying, but I didn't argue. I

mean, what was I going to do, watch him drive off without me? So, we stepped into his truck and rolled down the windows. He produced a bottle of cologne from the glove box, gave us each a spray, and tossed the bottle back into the glove box. We drove off into the night, laughing.

Charlie said that he needed to stop at a friend's house, which was on the other side of the park's panhandle. We soon parked in front of a huge Victorian house and approached its front door. Charlie knocked and told me to just act cool. Moments later, an orange-haired, pale-skinned, freckled-faced, thin-bodied chick answered the door with wide eyes. The wind blew her red and white cotton dress to one side, momentarily exposing her pinkish knees.

"Hey, baby, knew you'd finally come around to calling again," she said and hugged Charlie. "Who's this guy?"

"This handsome man is my best friend Jack."

She eyed me up and down in an inspecting kind of way, then looked at Charlie and said, "Yes, he is a looker, isn't he?" She shifted her eyes back to mine and introduced herself with an extended hand. "Hello, my name's Belle, come on in," she said, then turned and walked deeper into the dimly-lit house.

The house was cold and smelled of recently

cooked food, and it was sub-divided in to studio apartments with common areas, such as the kitchen, backyard, and selected bathrooms. As I followed them up three flights of threadbare-carpeted stairs, Belle and Charlie talked of things that were foreign to me, and I couldn't but wonder the reason for stopping at this odd house. On the third floor, Belle led us to her oddly-shaped room, which wasn't anything more than a converted attic space, but it was warm, cozy, and smelled of Nag Champa, and its oval-shaped window offered a great view of the panhandle.

As they talked, I blended into the background. Belle had decorated her room with strings of white and purple, Christmas lights, posters of The Clash, David Bowie, Velvet Underground, and The Rocky Horror Picture Show, and too many trinkets to name. A patchwork quilt covered her bed, which was nothing more than a single mattress on the floor. And as Belle rambled on, giving Charlie the latest updates on her life, she opened a wooden box that sat on a shelf and removed her pipe and a sandwich bag filled with Humboldt County weed. The place smelled of skunk, as she packed the bowl and took a hit.

Belle rested against a wall and, with pipe in hand, said, "I'm thinking of blowing this place, man. It's wearing me down, you know? It's changing around here. I think I'm one of the last still hanging on," she said, taking another hit.

"Seattle, man, that's where I'm going, already got people waiting for me. They rented a house with a backyard. Yeah, that's my plan, but I'm still working up the cash, though, might be another month or two…"

She and Charlie talked about people that I'd never met and of places I'd never been, so I tuned out and looked out the oval-shaped window. It was some minutes before she called my name. "Jack," she said, then offered me her pipe with a smile. I accepted and saw Charlie hand Belle some money. I took a big hit, coughed, coughed again, and passed the pipe to Charlie. Belle took the money, tucked it away in her brown leather purse, and apologized for not having any beer in her mini-fridge. She moved about her bedroom with precision and produced a mirror, razor blade, glass tooter, and a pile of cocaine. The next two hours were spent talking, listening to music, and doing drugs.

Later, on the porch, after we all finished our cigarettes, Belle gave us hugs, whispered something into Charlie's ear, and disappeared back into the house. I followed Charlie off the porch and into his truck and wondered how much cocaine we actually snorted in Belle's tiny room. Evening air poured into Charlie's truck, as we circled back to Haight Street.

I got the feeling that Charlie was stalling, because he kept talking about everything under the moon, except going to Mariposa Oscura, which only made me more curious. A few moments had passed before the coke got the best of me.

"What's your deal with driving around the same five blocks, Charlie? Don't say that you're looking for parking either, because I thought we're going to that club, man."

"That shit's getting to you, isn't it? I can tell, just look at you, all jacked up on that shit. I told you to take it easy, didn't I?"

"I'm high, no doubt, so what, but I not tripping on that."

"Oh, no? What then? What's got your goat, Jacky?"

"It's just that I thought we'd be drinking and bullshitting in a real club with fine women, not some slowpoke, dive bar, you know what I mean? That's all. It's no big deal, though."

Charlie smiled and said, "Well, for not being a big deal, you sure are bitching a lot about it. But, I guess you're right. I guess it's time for a freak show."

Charlie turned off Haight Street and darted down another street, making a few right and left turns onto several side streets, and we were moving so fast that I didn't even attempt to look at the street names, because it was pointless and my sense of direction was spinning and spinning like the needle in a broken compass, but I didn't care. I was drifting beneath pale-yellow, electric lights, beneath a dark sky filled with tattered fog and dying stars, and I was young and alive in San Francisco.

Charlie parked on a side street in the industrial side of town, and I assumed we were in walking distance to the Mariposa Oscura nightclub. We were surrounded by dilapidated warehouses, auto garages, and metal supply yards; and like the dark, dirty, outskirts of any city, I knew our safety was in jeopardy and any cry for help would fall on deaf ears. We walked a couple of blocks, and the city's energy crackled in the air.

Turning the corner onto a popular street, the rush of traffic raced to the perfect sequence of green lights. Cars, trucks, taxis, buses, limousines scattered and disappeared into the night. Daring pedestrians darted into the street and zigzagged like frightened cockroaches to avoid being crushed. On the next block, under a streetlight and a glowing business sign, three drunken teenagers skateboarded about and smoked marijuana, passing the joint as they passed each other. Their boisterous chatter bounced off a nearby building and died in the street. One of the teenagers ridiculed a homeless man who searched for food in a trashcan. A gust of wind picked up, quick, like an unexpected slap to the face, and flung specks of dirt into my eye; and from a nearby street, a trumpeter strung, slurred notes together in a way that made his horn weep in sorrow.

As Charlie and I crossed the street, we noticed small crowds of people buzzing about the sidewalk, tiny huddles of talkers and smokers, all carrying on; and tucked below the street chatter, with his hunched back against a building, an old man with sunglasses and crossed legs pressed his trumpet into his pursed lips, as if kissing a dear friend, and blew music for the broken-hearted. His notes swam into the air, like rain returning to the heavens, and evaporated, as though they were never there.

We had walked four or five blocks before reaching the line of people waiting to enter the Mariposa Oscura. Charlie mumbled something under his breath, but the middle-aged, leather-clad woman walking a skinny, semi-nude man on a leash captivated my attention. Charlie nudged me and delivered a grin that said, "You asked for this, didn't you?" I turned away and had second thoughts of entering the club. Most of the people in line wore S&M and gothic attire while some wore next to nothing. I scanned the front of the purple painted building for its name, wondering if we were at the right address, but nothing of a name was offered, only a "M" and an "O" were stenciled in black paint above the building's address. A small, neon sign of a purple butterfly trapped within a white circle hung above the entrance and glowed into the night.

"What's with the butterfly?," I asked, nodding at the sign, and then waiting for Charlie to exhale his smoke and answer.

In a whisper, he said, "That's the mariposa oscura, Jack. The dark butterfly."

The line began moving; and, one by one, people disappeared into the building. As I approached the entrance, I heard the beating of war drums and felt sonic rhythms vibrate throughout my body. While scanning the faces and bodies of those in line, reality blurred in and out of focus, slam dancing with surrealism, distorting and transforming into various familiar and unfamiliar images, all becoming primal, all dripping gasoline and waiting to be set on fire.

CHAPTER 14

Pink, blue, white, yellow, and purple beams of light ran across the dance floor, blurring into each other. They jumped on mural painted walls and climbed up to the ceiling like long-legged insects, crawling up and down, over and over, again. Green laser beams shot through the room, separating, intersecting, and fanning out with complete randomness. The air was thick and humid and smelled of perspiration and expensive fragrances. White lights strobed upon the walls, feverishly throwing blinding light onto shadowed faces, exchanging their fluidity for jerking, lurching movements. They appeared as human-like robots, drinking and laughing and dipping their heads in and out of pools of shadow and pulsating light. These strange faces resembled ones who hid in the boughs of trees rooted outside children's bedrooms, the ones who could only be seen in moonlight.

On a platform perched above the dance floor, a gangly, eerie-looking man stood hunched over turntables and controlled the industrial music blaring from the chain-suspended speakers. Scantly dressed men and women danced and gyrated about in semidarkness and engaged in lascivious acts. The ever-changing beams of lights burned away previous sexual inhibitions and bathed these shiny dancers in a transcendental experience. Charlie and I walked through the crowd toward the entrance floor bar.

Behind the bar counter, which resembled a stainless-steel operating table, six bartenders worked in a synchronic rhythm, appearing as a single body with six heads and twelve arms. Squirming bodies standing at the bar shouted drink orders at the bartenders and each exchange moved like cogs in a well-maintained machine. A carnival funhouse mirror hung behind the bar and casted out distorted images, and various types of insects and reptiles were housed in large mason jars with clear liquid on the flanking shelves. It was strangely odd, yet I wanted to see more and, perhaps, even step into the unknown.

"So, what do you think?," Charlie shouted with a nudge and handed me a beer. "It's like a circus in here, right? They're three floors. Two floors and a basement, really, but it's called a floor. Follow me." Charlie pushed his way through the crowd and stopped when we had a more intimate view of the dance floor. We listened to music, drank our beers, and watched the menagerie.

A bald, middle-aged, soft-bellied man dressed in a postman's uniform danced with a young man in a English-styled, schoolboy uniform; and next to them, a voluptuous lady with closed eyes, a hot pink mohawk, pink suspenders, and a clear plastic skirt swayed her hips to the music. She seemed as if she was in a trance, completely oblivious to the other dancers. A bare-chested, leather shorts wearing gentleman with a waxed, handle bar mustache aggressively groped another, who looked like his twin. The two, muscular men took turns grinding on each other's front and backsides and reminded me of thick-necked, leather strapped wrestlers looking to secure a tap-out headlock. My sights swiftly drifted across the floor and fell on a pair of beautiful, brunette women.

They wore red, latex, thigh-high boots with thongs to match, and each had two small, strips of black, electrical tape stretched across their nipples. As they danced, the taller of the two women slid her hand behind the other's back and took hold of her partner's ponytail. She spun her hand around the braided locks of hair and craned her partner's head back, gently yet dominantly, tilting her chin upward, exposing the softest section of her throat. The dominant woman stared into the other woman's eyes; and when the submissive broke the stare, the dominant woman drew closer and placed a vampire-like kiss on her partner's neck. I was mesmerized and left wondering if I had been the only witness to their moment.

"Are you thinking of asking them for a dance, Jack? Because, I don't think you're their type. Get what I'm saying?"

"What do you mean?"

"You got the wrong parts, Jacky," Charlie said, bouncing his eyebrows with a smile. "Stay put. I'll be right back. Time for a refill."

Charlie tossed his empty bottle into a nearby trashcan and disappeared into the crowd.

I watched on, floating my sights from the dance floor to the DJ, to the third floor, across the room, across unfamiliar faces and back, until I sensed I was being watched. My sights wandered the room again, low and high, scanning for prying eyes, but none were found, so they returned to the shiny dancers. And again, I felt a pair of eyes burning into me. I raise my eyes upward toward the third floor staircase, and there she was: a young, blond-haired woman in a red blouse staring down at me. As we held eye contact, time seemed to go on forever, but it was only a moment before she turned away and disappeared from my sight. I wondered if she was staring at me, or some other person standing behind me. I wanted to believe that it was I who captivated her attention, but I wasn't certain.

Toward the rear of the room, adjacent to the dance floor, I noticed a slender, platinum blond-haired lady sitting inside a steel cage, as if on display; and some feet beyond her, a leather-hooded man stood bound to a whipping post and received his share of flogging from a lanky, Asian dominatrix. She blew cigarette smoke in his direction and delivered heavy-handed strikes to his backside. The glowing red marks across his fleshy, white ass proved they were no strangers to this sort of fetish.

More people entered the club and poured onto the dance floor. And honestly, no one seemed taken aback by anything in the club, except the long wait for alcohol. Charlie soon returned with more drinks and complaints about the bartenders and pushy people at the bar. Because Charlie was a couple of inches shorter than most, he had developed a take-no-bullshit attitude to keep from being bullied. He mentioned that he had to rib someone at the bar who tried pushing him aside. He said this with a devilish grin.

I knew Charlie secretly enjoyed standing up to bullies, and what he lacked in height, he made up for in speed and strength. So, when he mentioned that he ribbed someone at the bar, I knew there was more to his story, and I was right. After Charlie handed me a beer, he showed me a leather wallet and handled it in a way that made me believe that the wallet wasn't his. Charlie emptied the wallet of its cash and offered me the wallet as a gift, but I had no interest in it, so he tossed the wallet in a trashcan and went back to drinking his beer.

Charlie took notice of the master and slave exchange and the caged woman in the distance, but didn't seem surprised. He said something about pink toilet paper with pretty, little flowers on it and then laughed. I laughed, too, but not because I heard what he said, but rather, because Charlie appeared so amused and wildly-eyed. We were drinking and having fun and not giving a shit about tomorrow. I was lost in the colorful moment. And, the more Charlie shouted his thoughts to me and gestured about, the more I laughed. Charlie gripped my shoulder, leaned into my ear, and told me to follow him downstairs before venturing into the crowd.

From a distance, under the shifting lights and green laser beams, the dancers' faces appeared semi-hidden behind cheap, plastic, transparent masks, glossy and artificial. I turned away and tracked Charlie through the club, as though I had tunnel vision, trying not to lose him in the moving crowd. He disappeared and reappeared while walking beyond a wall of drinkers at the bar, then weaved around more people on his way toward a far, dark corner of the room.

A gold-colored cherub with puckered lips spouted red liquid into a porcelain fountain basin, which rested several feet from an arch entrance. As Charlie approached the fountain, he disappeared within the crowd. There was no point in calling out to him, so I kept walking in his direction. Upon reaching the cherub fountain, the basement's entrance came in to view, which was a tunnel-like staircase leading downward with hanging lights bulbs to light the way. A painting of an old man and a centaur in a wooden dinghy hanged above the entrance, and the scent of ammonia entered the air. Charlie reappeared and said, "Follow me, and don't touch the handrail," then descended into the stairwell. As I trailed behind him, stepping deeper into the dark cavern, my ears popped and every sound became muffled, as if I was sitting at the bottom of a swimming pool.

The black walls appeared wet, as though they were freshly glazed. On the right side of the wall, words and illustrations were scrawled in gold paint by an uneasy hand. But as I took a closer look, I noticed that these weren't words at all; they were some type of hieroglyphics.

"When we get down there, don't worry if someone stares at you. They're just testing you," Charlie said, turning his chin to his shoulder.

"Testing me? For what?," I asked, nearly grabbing hold of the handrail.

"They want to see if you're scared, so stay relaxed, okay? They're just playing dress up," he said with a chuckle.

"Yeah, whatever. What's that smell? Smells like cat piss and latex."

"Disinfectant."

Up from the basement, just beyond a bend in the staircase, live music could be heard; and as the music grew louder, the temperature grew colder.

Reaching the bottom of the staircase, Charlie pointed to the words "The Playground," which were scratched into the wall, colored with yellow paint, and rested above the doorway. A pale, waif-like woman with orange hair and dressed in a white, two-piece, latex bikini stood tethered to a wall near the entrance. She smiled and mumbled something at us as we passed. Her black, dilated pupils floated within her eye sockets, and her red lipstick had smeared onto her a left cheek.

The crimson colored room was cold, and the fog machines created a stagnate layer up to one's knees. On a small stage, three musicians performed under red, green, and purple lights. A banner hanged behind the droning band with the words "Fiendishly Dying" hand-painted onto it.

Adjacent to the stage, another latex and leather clad couple performed S&M styled theatrics, which involved electronic and lacerating devices. We took our place near the tiny bar and watched razor lines appear on the hooded man's back. Moments later, a chubby, red-haired waitress in a torn, dirty wedding dress approached us and asked for our drink order. She smelled of body odor, cigarette smoke, and peppermint gum.

In the back of the room, on the opposite wall across from the stage, four booths were occupied by Dracula's coven. Some of them stared, as though we intruded on their congregation. "Look at these fucking guys, with their fake, pointy teeth, giving us the stare down treatment, drinking V8 juice, and pretending it's blood. Fucking Lestat wannabes. And, someone should really tell that fat kid in the corner that vampires don't have beer bellies and feed on pizza. They're supposed to be vampires for fuck's sake. I guess he won't be flying away with his friends tonight? Man, I got two words for these assholes: suck it!," Charlie said, then hissed like a cat while showing me his teeth. My shoulder muscles tightened, as I turned my back on them, but couldn't help laughing at Charlie's vampire impression.

"What the fuck? Vampire's aren't supposed to have mustaches, dude, especially ones like that," I said, curbing my laughter.

"No, man, that's the whole point. That's the genius in it, man. It makes my victims think they're safe. They're like, 'He's not a vampire. He can't be. He has a mustache,' then, out of nowhere, I'm like—"

Charlie hissed again and tried biting the top of my head. What a fucking idiot, but, man, I couldn't stop laughing.

Our waitress soon brought our drinks, but refused payment, because I reminded her of a boy she once dated in high school. "He was my first, believe it or not, and lately, I've been thinking about him more than usual; he's visited me in my dream twice this week," she confessed, leaning into us.

"He must've been real special if you still dream about him," I said, taking a sip of beer. "You should call him. I bet he'd love to hear your voice."

"I wish I could, really I do, but I can't," she said, allowing her shoulders to droop.

"Sure, you could, just pick up the phone and dial his number. Say you were thinking of him. Guys love that shit."

"He was killed by a drunk driver three days before our graduation."

A booth of thirsty vampires waved at her, wanting their drink orders taken.

137

"Gotta go. Enjoy your night, guys," she said and made her way toward the row of booths.

"Man, that shit was depressing. Sad and depressing, right?" Charlie said, waiting for my answer. "Right or what?"

"Charlie, you could be a real crass son of a bitch, sometimes. You know that?"

"Oh, come on, man. I mean, yeah, that's some fucked up shit, what happened to her boyfriend, but come on, Jack. We're here to drink and have a good time, not get our spirits thrown in the dumpster by some chick with a sad story, right? Besides, you want to know the real truth?"

"As opposed to the fake truth?"

"Shut up, you know what I meant. The real truth is that chick was feeling you out, seeing if you wanted her."

"What? You're fucking crazy, dude."

"No, man, I'm serious. Didn't you see how she got all misty eyed when she talked about her old boyfriend?"

"Yeah, that's because the dude got run over by a car, man, not because she wanted to have sex."

"See, that's where you're wrong, Jacky. She definitely wanted to have sex."

"With who, you?"

"No, man, not with me— with you, you, dumbass. She said that you reminded her of her old boyfriend, her first. That's chick code for the dude who took her virginity, and she still dreams of that guy."

"So?"

"So, if you reminded her of the lad who took her virginity, then she will gladly give you her pussy tonight. She wants to fuck you, Jack. Trust me; she definitely does. You should get laid or get her phone number at least, something. You're wide open and she threw you the ball. What are you going to do, Jack? Fumble or run it in for a fucking touchdown? Your choice. Who cares if she has B.O., dude? She wants you."

"You're seriously twisted, Charlie. I want you to know that. You should make a mental note of that. I love you, man, and you know that, but you a real jaded motherfucker, okay?"

Charlie looked at me long and hard, took a swig off his beer, and said, "Okay, I can live with that, but it still doesn't change the fact that that chick wants to fuck you, so she could fuck her old boyfriend, know what I mean?"

"Yeah, maybe, you're right. Fuck it. Who cares?"

"My point exactly. Who fucking cares?,"

Charlie said, and clinked my beer bottle. "Faith and friendship, Jack. That's all we got in this heartless world. Let's get the hell out of here."

After stepping our way up the staircase and pushing through the sweaty crowd, Charlie led me to another staircase, which was far narrower than the previous one. People used the right side of the stairs to ascend and the left to descend; and as we ascended, a blond-haired woman crashed into me, the one with the red blouse. When our eyes met and we were face to face, I felt the urge to say something, anything, but before I could utter a word, she was gone again. I watched her descend the stairs, trying to keep a sharp eye on her red blouse, but it was lost in a wash of color and people.

The staircase ascended to a lounge, which was furnished with purple and maroon colored sofas and oversized sky-blue chairs with white piping. Charlie located two of these chairs and pushed them closer together, so we could speak to each other without shouting. Large, gold-framed, Baroque-style paintings hanged on the walls and depicted pastoral landscapes. Like the chairs, there were also oval-shaped tables randomly placed about the floor, as if skirted aside from the people who gathered in front of the floor-to-ceiling windows.

From a distance, these lengthy windows gave the illusion that the south wall of this floor didn't exist, and people were drawn to them. The wall of glass allowed for a spectacular view of downtown. The myriad of white lights from the many skyscrapers permeated through the drifting, stretching fog, which at times resembled a gray, tattered scarf being pulled so thin that light moved through the fabric with ease. And farther in the distance, above the buildings and within the darkened sky, moonlight beamed in between traveling clouds. I sensed that Charlie wasn't ready to take a breather from the brimming excitement below. He fidgeted some and grew antsy. I knew he wanted to snort more coke, and within three minutes another bump found its way to each of our noses.

"Man, let's get out of here; my farts are leaving warm. I'm not sure if it's the blow or the bean and cheese burritos we ate, but I need to take a shit, like now, dude," Charlie said, standing from the chair and offering a bill. "Here's a hundred, get us some drinks, top shelf, and meet me by the fountain on the main floor, you know where it is, right?"

"Yeah, by the cat piss staircase," I said and pocketed the cash.

"Alright, I'll meet you there, and whatever you do, don't get adventurous, just stay put, okay?," Charlie said and darted off and down the staircase and into the shifting crowd.

CHAPTER 15

Humidity rose off the dance floor and travelled midway up the staircase. As I descended, dampness wrapped itself around me like a musty, leather trench coat, and the crowd of sexually charged people swarmed about, but I managed to push my way through the sea of PVC, latex, and leather, but not without being groped several times. As I stood at the bar, more like wedged against it, something repeatedly bumped into my backside; however, when I looked behind me, every face waiting at the bar appeared oblivious to what was occurring in the waist deep shadows.

The crowd swayed and moved in all directions and mixed with pulsating music, shouting voices, random and anonymous groping, hot, lascivious, and unmentionable acts huddled together under a colorful, brick and mortar umbrella, while foul and pleasing scents swirled together and travelled about the room on invisible wings. The crowd surged again and again, like blood passing through a partially clogged artery.

I held the cash in one hand and used the other to brace myself against the bar; and again, an unseen hand slid up my inner thigh and over my groin and was gone. When one of the bartenders pointed to me, I began shouting my drink order; however, before I could finish, the beautiful woman in the red blouse crashed into me; and this time, she smiled in a way that led me to think that our proximity wasn't accidental. Before the bartender had a chance to finish the drinks, I felt someone step on my foot, press an elbow into my back, and pluck the hundred-dollar bill from my fingers.

I spun around and saw the woman in the red blouse standing just out of my reach. She held up the C-note and waved, much like one does to a dog with a toy. I lunged toward her and tried grabbing the bill from her hand, but she reeled it back. At that moment, the crowd shifted direction again; and with her limber body and cunning movement, she drifted toward the main exit. She turned back to see if I was following her, and I was, which caused her to smile again.

As I approached the exit, I noticed her standing outside, waiting. Our eyes met once more, as I saw her climb into the backseat of a taxi. I staggered out of the club and into the taxi without thought. The taxi driver tore away from the curb so fast I hardly had a chance to close the door.

"What the hell are you doing?," I questioned, but the woman didn't say a word. She just sat there in the backseat, calm and collect, as if nothing had happened, so I continued ranting, but it wasn't making any sort of impact on her. She only spoke to the driver, giving specific driving directions. He steered the taxi through the city, making lefts and rights, and disregarded me as well, leading me to ask, "What is this?"

It was only when I gripped the driver's shoulder and demanded that he stop the car and let me out did the woman say, "Relax, baby, don't ruin it; it's all in the name of fun and mystery. You like mystery, don't you?"

"Listen, whatever your name is—"

"It's Delilah."

"Whatever. Tell this fucking guy to stop the car, give me back the cash, and we could be done with this, whatever *this* is, alright?"

"Ah, don't be like that, baby. Be nice. Be a sweetheart, please," she said and placed her hand on my leg just above my knee; and with a tiny squeeze, she again said, "Please. This is supposed to be fun. And, it will, if you relax and just let it happen. Tell me what to call you. You can be anyone tonight, just tell me…"

As she spoke, a pale, white light entered through the backseat window and danced in her green eyes. They were captivating unlike any other. Her pupils dilated and her lips parted slowly, saying words that never reached my ears; and, as we drove onward, she smiled in such a way that I became lost somewhere in between the past and present. And, even though, I'd never met this person until now, there was something oddly familiar about her, as though I'd known her for years.

"Call me Jack. Where are we going?"

She stared at me with curious eyes and held a silly smirk, giggled a bit, and said, "I just told you. Weren't you listening, Jack?"

"Of course, I was. I was seeing if you—"

"Oh, I get it; you're a tricky one. You were seeing if I was what?"

"To tell you the truth, I can't even remember. Doesn't matter anyway, does it? Fuck it. It's all fun and mystery at this point, right?"

"Now, you're catching on."

She took a deep breath, stroked her blond strands of hair, and exhaled. "Stop in front of the brown building, the one with the red and green flags," she said, straightening her posture. The driver pulled to the side of the street and, before he could state the fare, Delilah tossed a crumpled bill in to the front seat and stepped out of the taxi. She trotted toward a glass door, which stood protected behind an elaborately designed wrought iron security gate. I trailed behind, following her up several steps, into the apartment building lobby, and into a waiting elevator. It must have been the dumbfounded look on my face that solicited her answer. "Yes. Don't look so surprised. Where did you think I lived? No, don't answer that," she said, as the elevator doors closed.

I wondered why she snatched the money from my hands, because anyone as young as her who could afford to live in such an impressive apartment building wasn't in need of a measly hundred dollars. Maybe, she didn't want to go home alone or, perhaps, she wanted to be seen leaving with someone. Whatever her reason was for taking the money, it was anyone's guess. Maybe, this is what she meant when she said, "It's all in fun and mystery."

CHAPTER 16

Her perfume invaded the elevator space, and there was an uncomfortable silence between us. "How often does she do this?," I wondered, as her stare ricocheted off the fine-polished elevator doors and pierced my eyes, searching for something unknown. Her soft, feminine face held red lips so delicately shaped that I couldn't imagine that they ever spoke of awful things. Strangely, I felt as though I was a teenager again, but I knew better. This wasn't prom night or anything like that.

This was Russian roulette of some sort: I'd been chosen for one reason or another, the lucky one who gets the bullet in the chamber, then in the head. I hoped that it was all going to be worth it in the end, but most of us know, it rarely is. However, I had ventured too far to turn back, and the money was now nothing more than a fleeting thought. I had to know what she was thinking for us, what was the next step in her little plan of fun and mystery, or was this a random game of charades? The doors opened on the fourth floor, and she stepped out as she'd done a million times before, and there was noticeable confidence in her stride. The scent of fresh flowers lingered in the hallway.

Her jingling keys spiked above the muffled sounds escaping from the behind the row of doors. She looked over her shoulder before stopping and keying open her door. "Come in and have a drink," she offered, walking into her place. "There's plenty to chose from. Come, Jack. Come." She now spoke with a fading European accent, which was strange because I didn't notice it in the taxi; and as she continued, her accent faded in and out, only making itself known with certain words, as though she had speech training to lose her mother tongue.

She walked into the restroom without concern, and I waited for her on the leather sofa. Lithographs, mostly of Picasso's Blue Period, hanged on the walls. Across the largest wall, moving from left to right, soft light washed on a triad of lithos, and each one had a gold seal upon it, displaying the artist's name, the title of the work, and the year the work was created. The three read: *Pablo Picasso. Blue Nude, 1902*; *Pablo Picasso. Woman and Child by the Sea, 1902*; *Pablo*

Picasso. The Tragedy, 1903. I figured I would use Picasso to open the conversation. And, it was better than saying, "Hey, shut your tired mouth, and give me my money." She was taking her sweet time in the restroom, so I assumed she was making herself sweet for me, and I didn't mind.

However, I was getting bored, had cottonmouth, and needed a drink. Across the bearskin rug, past a bunch of houseplants and the entertainment center, the booze cart smiled at me and said, "Hello." "Well, hello, there, sweetie; that's where she keeps you," I said under my breath and walked over for a drink.

Delilah reappeared some moments later, just as I was capping the bottle of scotch. She moved toward me with her hand extended, as though wanting to shake my hand. I offered her my hand and said, "Jack Marshall." She smiled then chuckled. "I was reaching for my drink, silly," she said.

"Right. Lucky, I made two. Scotch," I said, handing her a glass.

"Something tells me you're kindhearted, are you?," she asked, taking a drink. "Like this drink says you have manners but don't believe in soda water."

"Sorry. I try. I mean, I try to be kind, sometimes. Not exactly sure. Do you think I am?"

"I have my suspicions, but I hope that you're not, not too much, anyway."

She took a drink, eyeing me over the rim of her glass, and nothing more needed to be said. I discovered that her last name was Kincade and she mentioned something about an uncle and his rich friends and how they all knew each other from the university. I'll tell you the truth, at that moment, I didn't give a shit about her stories. I couldn't have cared less, but I pretended to seem interested, because that's what people do in these types of situations; it's a little social game we all learn to play to some degree. I wondered of her age and assumed it to be around mine, give or take a year, but it's unwise to assume anything merely based on appearances.

"Are you still upset about the money, darling? Tell me that you're not, okay? I know I can be a bitch at times, but all I was trying to do was have fun. I hope you weren't put off by it too much. Are you?"

"No, not really, not at the moment."

"Good. I'm glad you followed me. I really am. It shows you go after what's yours, even if it is a handful of pennies. It's so American, another pride thing, I suppose. Remind me to return it before you leave, okay?"

"Sure."

"So, do you like it, darling?"

I had no clue of what she was referring to, so I said the first thing that entered my mind.

"Yeah, I do like it. Always have, you know?"

She just looked at me for a moment, dumbfounded, as though I answered in an unknown language. I feigned cool, confident, and took a drink from my glass. Her tiny smile grew in to a giggle, and then in to a laugh, that became so infectious that I began laughing as well. And through her laughter, she asked, "What do you like about it?"

Again, my drunken mind scrambled for an answer to an unknown subject; and as I sat speechless, thoughts reeling, she prodded me again. "Do tell, I wish to know. Go on, what do you like about it, Jack?"

"Well, who wouldn't like it, I mean, right? It's, it's, really, I don't know. What's the word for it? I've heard it before, but— what's the word?"

She burst in to a fit of laughter, placing her arm over stomach, and said, "The word? You wish to know the word for it?"

"Yeah, you know it. What is it?"

"Bullshit! It's bullshit, Jack. That's what it is."

She regained her composure, dried the corners of her eyes, grabbed the glass from my hand, and asked, "Another drink, yes?"

"Yes."

"This I know is no lie," she said, chuckling a bit as she walked across the room. "You're very funny. Funny, funny, and I miss that so much. Everybody is always so stern and serious, but life isn't meant to be lived that way. It's meant to be lived with—"

"Fun and mystery?"

"Yes. Exactly, Jack. Fun and mystery. That is it. Let's drink to it, okay?"

And, we did.

Delilah handed me another scotch and asked if we could continue our conversation on the balcony. And, of course, I agreed. The thought of her apartment having a balcony never entered my mind, because the glass door leading to the balcony was hidden behind a pair of heavy, brown curtains, but I enjoyed the idea. We stepped onto the balcony with our drinks in hand and drank in the magnificent view of the bay. The evening air was crisp, to say the least, but was reduced to an afterthought. "Isn't it beautiful?," she said, turning on an outdoor heater. "It would be perfect, if it wasn't so cold, absolutely perfect."

From where I stood, I saw tops of houses and buildings, headlights moving through city streets, colorful signs, and traffic lights; and as I followed them, my eyes were led out to the black waters of the bay and across to Sausalito. "I could never grow tired of it. It's amazing."

"On a clear night, the bridge will come in to view, and on a windy night, much windier than tonight, you can hear the faint sound of a cable car's bell being struck. It rides on the wind, you know, comes in, sometimes," she said, taking a drink. "Without sounding too weird, I would like to ask you a question, do you mind?"

"No, go ahead, ask away," I said, turning toward her.

"Would you believe me if I said the stars brought us together?"

"The stars, huh?"

"Yeah, but not like 'The Stars,' like you said it, not like how a crazy person says 'The Stars, like, far out, man, give me more drugs, man. Wow, look, the stars, man,' not like that," she said, playfully showing me her small fist. "Not like that, but like, you know, like destiny or whatever, something like that— the stars, you know? It could be true, couldn't it? Just because I don't know the right word for it, Jack, doesn't mean that I don't know what I'm talking about, because I do, it exists. It's out there...."

At times, as she spoke, everything would go silent, as though I had become momentarily deaf, making my sight my only functioning faculty. Her green eyes had an innocence and unusual nature to them, as if granted the captivating power of drawing one closer to her, almost hypnotizing in a way, and it was how she looked at me, more like, through me, that made me wonder if she was once like me, having spent her adolescent years in a place with nothing on the horizon other than the setting sun.

And as we drank, we spoke to each other with a candidness that longtime friends only share, but it's the fact that we weren't longtime friends, or true friends, for that matter, that I believe made it easier for us to speak so openly with each other. We were perfect strangers, more or less, and that sort of anonymity allows for unbridled truth to surface with ease. We knew for the most part, that night, in those passing hours, was all we were ever going to have with each other. And it made no difference to us, because we were young, carefree, and living in the moment without regret. We were free to be anything or anyone we wanted to be.

"You have a beautiful smile, darling. You should use it more often, Jack. It's amazing what a person can receive with a simple smile, beautiful or not. Believe me. I know this to be true," she said and then flashed a smile so alluring, yet so automatic, it was like she had flicked on a smile switch, as if she had rehearsed that smile a million times over; but with her softened eyes, her white-teethed smile appeared unquestionably sincere. "Let me see your smile again," she requested.

"Like this?"

"No, not that way, more teeth, show more teeth, like this, darling. Try again."

"How's this? Is this better?"

"No. I said, 'More teeth.' Show more of your smile, more teeth. See, like this, Jack. See. No teeth. Now, with teeth. Now, with more teeth. More teeth looks better, right? And, do this with your eyes, like you have really long eyelashes."

"Yes, okay, it does look better, but I'm not sure if I can get my eyes and teeth to—"

"Shhh, try again, okay. Go."

I smiled and smiled, over and over again, trying my hardest to show more teeth and flutter my eyes, until she laughed so hard that not a sound was heard coming from her mouth. Then, it dawned on me: she used me for her amusement, had me making silly faces to make her laugh, but I didn't mind in the least. I rather enjoyed seeing her laugh, so I made more funny faces and mocked her instructions. "More, darling, more, like this," I said and fluttered my eyelashes, blinking them uncontrollably. We laughed until we weren't laughing at all, but instead, gazing in to each other's eyes. She tenderly bit her lower lip, moved closer to me, so close that the heat from her breath broke upon my mouth; and when her eyes met mine again, we closed them and kissed.

I floated in a black sea of white stars, spinning and surrounded in her touch, desiring something I've never experienced before. Her body felt more delicate than it appeared, and my hands explored regions without restrictions. Her breath quickened upon my neck, as her body tensed and relaxed and tensed again. "Wait, I'll be right back," she said, breaking from our embrace.

"Where are you going?," I asked, turning toward her silhouette.

She entered the apartment and removed her shoes.

"I'll only be a minute. Turn off the heater and come inside."

"Only a minute, not a second longer," I said, returning every thing to how we found it.

She giggled and began undressing, leaving a trail of clothes behind her, each garment leading to the restroom. "Pour us another drink. Would you?," she said, disappearing into the restroom. The sound of running water washed away my response, making it lost somewhere between my mouth and her ears, but it made no difference.

The alcohol was working well, and there was plenty of it in the apartment. For a moment, as I freshened our drinks, I wondered of Charlie, but dismissed the thought, believing he was safe and in the warm company of a wild woman. I wondered if Delilah was a wild woman herself. How often does this woman have one-night-stands with strangers? I would never know the truth, and maybe, it was for the best. I mean, I didn't even know if Delilah Kincade was her true name, and it didn't matter. Fuck it. What does any of it matter at this point? I brought the bottle to my lips and pulled a shot from it and felt it burn all the way down.

The shower water stopped, and the restroom door opened enough for her voice to escape. "There's some cocaine in the cabinet, under the television, darling. Can you set some out for us? It's Peruvian," she said, then closed the door again. Moments later, she appeared with nothing more than a lavender colored bath towel. Her fair skin radiated and her green eyes gleamed, as if they were made from glass. I knew exactly where this charade was now leading, but I couldn't help but feel a bit awkward about it, because it wasn't like this sort of thing happened to me all the time; in fact, this had never happened to me; although, I had imagined it many times. "The water's still hot, and there's a towel on the counter," she said with a seductive smile.

After my shower, I returned to the living room with only a white towel around my waist and noticed that Delilah was now completely naked. She slid something under the sofa and dimmed the lights. "The water must've tenderized the nick above your eyebrow. Come here and let me fix you up," she said, patting the spot where she wanted me to sit. I sat down next to her on the furry, black, bearskin rug. She dabbed my cut with her towel, leaving blood spots on the lavender cloth; and when she asked how I came to receive the wound, I lied. She began kissing my face; and again, everything started to feel dreamlike: I saw us naked on the floor, kissing and caressing each other, as though we'd been lovers forever.

Then, she handed me a mirror with the longest lines of cocaine on it that I had ever seen and made a line disappear, and so did I. The powder shot up my nose, fast and smooth; and as it drained, the cocaine coated and numbed the back of my throat. Within minutes, all but two lines remained on the mirror, resting next to a small pile of untouched coke. Delilah stood and her firm ass barely jiggled, as she approached the entertainment center. She turned on the television and pressed another button that started a porno movie, but there was no sound. She had muted the television's audio, so that romantic, instrumental music could be heard instead. I believed we were listening to Kenny G, but I wasn't sure, and I didn't care, because she turned, faced me, and swayed her body seductively. Her hands moved about her body, outlining every curve, and her eyes remained locked with mine.

"Do you think I'm beautiful, Jack?," she asked, gliding her hand down her inner thigh.

Her eyes held a hint of vulnerability within them.

"Yes, of course, you are."

I smoothed back my wet hair from my face.

"Then, why don't you tell me that I am, darling? Tell me. I want to hear you say it," she said, slowly raising her chin.

"You are beautiful. I thought you were beautiful from the moment I first saw—"

She entwined her arms in a way, as though questioning my sincerity.

"Am I beautiful enough to be more than what I am?"

I had no clue of what she was asking, but I did not falter.

"Of course, you are. We can always be more than what we are."

"There was a time when I believed that, but that was long ago. I want to believe that there's still time for something better."

"We all do, Delilah."

"I want to believe, darling."

She closed her eyes and danced, losing herself in the moment, as though no one existed in the world, but her, like a beautiful marionette cut free from its controlling strings. I watched and thought on how she had acquired all of her worldly luxuries. Perhaps, she was an exotic dancer, but I wasn't convinced. Her taste was too refined for that line of work: high-end apartment; designer clothes; fine furnishings; fine alcohol; Peruvian cocaine, and Picasso lithos on her walls. Maybe, she's an upscale escort, a wealthy man's mistress, or comes from money, trust money, perhaps, perhaps; anything was plausible. But one thing was certain, most woman her age would find it extremely difficult, if not near impossible, to financially compete with her. More interesting, was how she had little respect for purchased items and yearned for something with greater significance, something magnificently special.

When she opened her eyes and noticed that I still wore my towel, she said, "Modest, are we?" I released the towel, allowing it unfurl upon the floor. She licked her lips, produced a tube of lubricant, and whispered, "Now, it's my turn to watch you." She reclined against the sofa, legs splayed and hands gently moving, exploring her body. I moved closer, watching her erotically gliding her fingers up and down and in between her thighs in a slow and even fashion. I struggled at controlling the surging rush of carnal excitement as we enticed each other.

Whispering, Delilah told me to stand above

her so that my legs straddled her hips and to drip lubricant onto her body. She waited for several drops to collect on her stomach and areolas before massaging them into her skin. I bent down and kissed her shoulder, working my way toward her supple neck and left ear. Her hot breath warmed my skin, as she asked for me to bring her toys from her bedroom. "Everything's in the trunk," she whispered. "Whatever you wish, darling." I wandered into the hallway toward a nearby room, leaving Delilah in motion, as musical notes swirled throughout the apartment.

Delilah's four-poster bed rested in between two, louvered, closet doors, making it the centerpiece in the room. I looked around the room, but couldn't locate the trunk she had mentioned moments ago, which was strange, because everything in her bedroom seemed to be methodically placed. Granted, this was my first time in her bedroom, and I was feeling the effects of the booze and drugs, but I didn't think I would have to search for a piece of furniture. It was only when I stepped beyond her wardrobe that the antique trunk appeared. It was neatly hidden in plain sight.

As I kneeled down and opened the lid, I heard her say, "Jack, are you lost, darling? I'm waiting." Looking into the trunk, I discovered an array of adult toys. There was no denying that Delilah had a penchant for kinky sex. There were condoms, vibrators, lubricants, handcuffs, paddles and blindfolds, leather and chain mail apparel, and various types of restraint devices; all for S&M styled sex. To be embarrassingly honest about it, there were items in the trunk that I had never seen before and hadn't a clue how exactly they were to be used.

"Wait for me, just a minute longer," I said and then discovered a Polaroid camera. I moved aside a few more items, noticed something sticking out beyond a tear in the trunk's fabric lining, and found a thin stack of pictures wedged into one of the trunk's corners. As I quickly flipped through the stack, the disturbing images were a clear indication of why the photos were neatly tucked out of sight. The photographs were mostly of nude men, mostly older, white men in compromising positions; they were strapped and bound and bent into sexual positions. There were also images of group sex with men and women performing mascochistic and sadomachistic acts. Most of the pictures had the same man in them, the same face appearing over and over again. Then it hit me: I recognized this man. I knew his face. "But from where?," I wondered. I returned the photographs, grabbed a few items, and closed the lid. As I turned to leave the bedroom, there was heavy-handed knock on the front door.

Delilah cursed the interruption and told me to remain in her room. "Sorry, this should only take a moment, darling," she said, walking toward the door. I'd never felt so humble as I did at that moment: I was standing in a stranger's bedroom, completely naked, holding two, rather large, rubber dildos, a couple of condom packets, and a bottle of lavender-scented lubricant in my hands. I wondered if Delilah had led me into some sort of trap, as I waited and listened cautiously.

I felt the door open, footsteps enter into the living room, and the door close. Delilah spoke jovially to a man who had a husky voice. I assumed she knew this person, perhaps a neighbor or a friend, because she sounded calm and comfortable. I exhaled, looked about the room, and wanted to sit down on the bed, but I didn't, fearing it would make noise.

I couldn't hear everything that was being said, only bits and fragments of their conversation. At moments, some of their words were quite clear; other times, they blended into the music and were lost. I stepped closer to the doorway to better eavesdrop on them. That's when I noticed the man spoke with an accent of some kind and told Delilah that she must return home and something about a campaign and liabilities. It seemed apparent that he no longer wanted her around. However, when Delilah laughed and refused his recommendation, he raised his voice and spoke with a stern tone. "I'm sure you completely understand what's in jeopardy here, do you not, Natalya?," he said. No words were spoken for a moment, before he continued. "And, of course, all of your expenses will be taken care of, as always. Be a good girl and go home."

His heavy footsteps moved across the living room floor with hers following. More words were spoken between them, but they were muffled beyond comprehension. However, when he told her that her travel arrangements would be made and that someone would see her to the airport, she laughed at him again.

"See me off, is that it? As if I am a child. Oh, and, I suppose you or another one of his little puppets will see me to the terminal, so that I don't get lost. Mustn't run the risk of missing my flight."

"Now, now, let's not be unreasonable. You knew the arrangement. It's run its course, and you were well compensated for your—"

"My what? What exactly was I 'compensated' for?"

"Lower your voice, Natalya. Please, I'm asking you nicely, okay? Please be civil."

"You're pathetic! I hardly see you fit to carry my bags. And, it's completely absurd that you'd believe for an instant that I'd listen to your petty demand, your so-called request."

"Natalya. Please."

"You're nothing more than a second-rate errand boy. I'll speak to Edward myself. Get out."

He apologized and lowered his voice, as if attempting to calm her. Again, she told him to leave her apartment and threatened to call Edward. She moved across the floor in a sure-footed fashion. Heavy steps followed. They began arguing again, but it soon ended with Delilah being slapped and the telephone being thrown to the floor. I recoiled, wondering what I should do, and scanned the room for a weapon, but there was nothing in sight, except a pair of ceramic candleholders. Panic now surged within me.

I held my breath, feeling my heartbeat in my throat, and heard a muffled scream and a brief struggle, all ending in a lifeless thump. Another male voice entered the living room, and I questioned if he had been there the entire time. I would never know for certain. Perhaps, he stood in the hallway, outside of the front door, waiting. One of the men walked to the stereo and raised the volume. My heartbeat raced in my ears and sweat had built on the back of my neck. I wondered if Delilah or Natalya or whoever she was was still alive. I wanted to believe that she was still breathing, but I suspected that she wasn't. Something within me said that the man had snapped her neck or choked the life right out of her. But again, I could only speculate; there was only one thing that I could be certain of: the two men didn't know I was in the apartment.

I remained motionless, waiting and listening, as I knew it would only be a matter of time before they searched the bedroom. Approaching the bed, I emptied my hands and hid the sex toys under a pillow. The music had swallowed the men's voices whole, making it difficult to discern what they were doing in the living room. I had to hide and do it quickly; I knew my life depended on it.

The men now could be heard moving about the apartment, shuffling objects around, as thieves would. They approached the mouth of the hallway and stopped, perhaps, removing the lithographs from the walls. They spoke in short, deep, tones, not words that I heard. It wasn't until a song ended that I clearly heard one man say something about a cocaine overdose and "Ed's worried about the collateral damage." This obviously made no sense to me, but there was no denying that I was at the wrong place at the wrong time. I had collateral damage written all over me, and I was naked, trapped, and cornered without a weapon. My clothes still remained on the hook behind the bathroom door, and I prayed that they would stay unnoticed. Three options came to mind. One, I could try to escape from the fourth story window, providing the window wasn't jammed. Two, simply walk out of the bedroom with nothing more than God's blessing.

Or, three, I could find a place to hide.

The pair of footsteps crossed the living room floor and entered the kitchen. Again, they began searching for something, opening and closing drawers and cabinets. In the process, one of the men knocked over glassware, a drinking glass or a bottle, because something shattered on the floor, which upset the other man. His monotone spiked and dropped into an even tone again.

While they exchanged tones, I thought of hiding under the bed, but decided to hide behind the louvered, closet doors instead. At least, this way I would be able to see the men as they entered the room. An image of police officers dragging my dead, naked body out from the closet bled into my mind, but I figured what the hell, if I was going to be a sitting duck, I'd rather be one behind a door than one under a bed. Fuck it. It was the better choice of the two, which wasn't a real choice at all.

Sitting on the floor, my back against the wall and in the dark, the smell of Delilah's stale perfume filled the closet. I reached above my head, pulled her clothes over me, and proceeded to camouflage myself in to a pile of dirty laundry. Each tiny sound that I made was amplified a thousand times louder in my imagination. I felt I was on the verge of vomiting, because I knew that I could be killed at any moment. I feared the sound of my breathing would give me away; as more beads of sweat collected upon my brow, making the dry cleaning bags stick to my face, a pair of heavy footsteps vibrated the apartment's floor. The vibrations increased with each approaching step. They were felt stepping through the living room, down the hallway, and into the bedroom.

The husky voiced man entered the bedroom and stopped, then began opening and closing dresser drawers. From the small space in between each louver, I saw his large shadow on the floor. The sound of finely sanded wooden boards sliding against each other was heard, as he searched each drawer. When he finished, he turned around and stood still, as though he knew I was in the room. He coughed several times and then took a step forward toward the bed. This wide-bodied man wore gloves and dark clothes. Nothing more could be seen from my position.

He kneeled and looked under the bed; this was when I noticed the man was white, middle-aged, and balding. He removed two boxes from beneath the bed, but found nothing of interest, then discovered the trunk. I heard him lift the trunk's lid. He stuck his arm into the trunk and searched about, but soon dismissed the contents. "Tools of the trade; what a little, stupid whore you turned out to be, darling. Poor, dead, darling," he said, allowing the trunk's lid to drop shut. He stood, cracked his knuckles into his palms, and remained motionless. His breathing had accelerated and caused him to cough several more times.

He searched the nightstand drawers and again found nothing, then shuffled around to the other side of the bed and did the same. "I know you have them, whore," he whispered. "I know you do." He opened the closet door with disregard and moved her clothes in a frustrated fashion, before kicking open a few of her shoeboxes. He was the closest he'd ever been to me. I was panic-stricken and nearly blacked out, and beads of sweat found their way into my eyes. I saw myself being strangled beneath this man's stare. When he searched her coat pockets and found nothing, he backhanded a nightstand lamp and sent it crashing to the floor. I tucked myself into the smallest form I possibly could and waited for him.

His footsteps slowly made their way back toward the other side of the bed again, and as he placed his hand on the closet door handle, the other man entered the room and said, "Did you find anything?"

"Not yet, but they must be here," he answered, opening the door halfway.

"Everything's in place. We must leave."

"But, I know they're here. Somewhere. One more minute, okay?"

"We're wasting time. We've already been here longer than we expected. Let's go."

The heavy-footed man stood two feet away from me and hastily parted a few clothes hangers before saying, "Fine by me, but you're telling Edward that we didn't find the photographs. Let's get out of here." Then, he followed the other man out of the bedroom.

In the living room, the men exchanged tones, and then nothing was felt or heard in the apartment, nothing except the music and the men's exiting footsteps. After the closing of the front door, the place felt lifeless. I remained hidden for another three or four minutes, which seemed like an eternity, before I crawled out from beneath the pile of clothes and opened the closet door. My hands shook uncontrollably. I struggled to regulate my shallow breathing while stretching out beyond the closet and onto the bedroom floor. If I didn't know any better, I would've believed that an automobile engine rested on my chest.

When I got to my feet, I lumbered out of the bedroom, down the hall, and into the bathroom. Everything moved in frames, like snapshots from a high-powered 35mm camera with an endless supply of film, and the hands that dressed me in the semi-dark room appeared to be controlled by someone other than myself, working fast and accurately about my body. It was only when I repeatedly splashed cold water on my face that I regained enough clarity to venture toward the living room.

Upon entering the living room, I saw Delilah's dead body lumped over on its side. The horrific sight caused my stomach to heave to the point of almost vomiting. A syringe stuck out from her arm and vomit-like foam had collected around her mouth. She had lost all control of her bodily functions. The men had left a burning candle next to a pile of heroin or cocaine; a bent, well-used spoon rested by the white powder, just an arm's length from Delilah's reach. As I stepped closer, I noticed that Delilah's green eyes were still open, frozen in to a death stare. My knees weakened, and the room started spinning. I held onto one of the column speakers for support, knocking over a fern plant onto the floor. A high-pitched ringing engulfed my hearing, as I stared at the fresh soil fanned out onto the floor. My knees buckled and my stomach erupted.

As I stood hunched over, swallowing back a mouthful of vomit, a small camcorder came in to view. It sat hidden behind the speaker, next to the fallen fern. The camcorder's red light was on, indicating that it was still recording. A sharp pain struck within my chest. I reached for the camcorder and pressed the "stop" button. The muted moans and erotic facial expressions still played on the television screen. All my thoughts became warped and distorted. The little bit of clarity that I had some moments ago was now lost again. The porno on the television, the thrown telephone, the romantic music in the air, and the dead body in the room and all the rest were too much for me to bear. I grabbed the camcorder and left the apartment.

In the hallway, as I approached the elevator, everything felt unnaturally slow, surreal, like the whole world was spinning in an underwater dream. The elevator was in between floors, so I darted toward the door leading to the stairs. As I descended, I thought of countless scenarios that linked me to Delilah's murder, which was obviously constructed to appear as anything but a murder, but rather a drug overdose or suicide. When I reached the ground floor, I composed myself and entered into the lobby. The last thing I wanted to do was attract attention to myself.

The lobby was quiet, and my sights were like lasers on the exit. I couldn't run the risk of being placed at the scene of the crime. At that moment, I wanted nothing more than to disappear into the night, as if I had never existed. My exit would have been so clean it could've rivaled a ghost's, except for the drunken, middle-aged couple who staggered into me on the street. "Watch where you're going, you fucking asshole," the man slurred, as I scrambled away into the darkness.

CHAPTER 17

A thick fog layer had rolled in, blanketing the city, and my main objective was to place great distance between Delilah's body and me. I had no sense of direction. I could've been walking down any random street in the world, because everything appeared foreign to me. When I looked over my shoulder, all I saw was a brownstone building with two flags, one red and one green. That's it. Everything else blurred beyond recognition. In my mind, each pair of approaching, blinding headlights belonged to police cars. Panic surged each time headlights appeared on the street. I turned down another street and jogged for a few minutes. Police sirens wailed somewhere in the nearby distance, and I believed they were looking for me. That's when I began a conversation with myself, which was nothing more than a feeble attempt to rationalize what had occurred some minutes ago.

"You're paranoid, Jack. That's all there is to it. Get a hold of yourself, man. Do you hear me? Just calm the fuck down. They're just sirens. They're not looking for you. Are you listening? No one knows where you came from or what you've seen tonight. Nobody. Jack, are you fucking listening?"

"Yeah. No. No, wait a minute. This is all bullshit. She's dead, and I'm linked to her murder. Linked, one way or another. I could've helped her. I could've helped save her life. I… I helped— I helped them kill her, didn't I?"

"Get a hold of yourself. You're all over the place. You kept yourself alive, Jack. That's what happened. Consider yourself lucky, because, by all odds, you should be dead in that apartment. You survived. That's what happened."

"But, I was there. My fingerprints are all over that place. My goddamn DNA, it's on her body, for Christ sakes. I'm on her dead body! On her neck, on her ears, on her mouth— everywhere. And, my blood is on her towel. I'm not—"

"It's circumstantial and—"

"Circumstantial? Are you fucking kidding me? They're going to put me in prison for something I didn't do. That's how it fucking works. And, you know what? I'm not going to rot away in some rat hole, alone and forgotten. I didn't kill her. That much I know."

"You didn't kill her. That's exactly right, but the evidence will prove that you were with her tonight. There's no doubt about that, but it doesn't prove that you murdered her. You can still go to the police and explain everything, even why you left the scene of the crime."

"This is all too much. I can't think. Fuck! No, if I go to the cops, they'll already have evidence to build a case against me. You know how they work."

"If you tell them all you know, and if they find the murderers, and if the D.A. believes you, then you have nothing to worry about. It's still not too late, Jack."

"Let me get this straight. My DNA on a dead woman's body, a story about the actual murderers, and a fresh-off-the-farm public defender? That's the deal?"

"And, the truth. Just tell the truth."

"Even if I had the money for a great lawyer, I'd never escape this shit. It'd follow me for the rest of my life, everywhere I go, and the media... my life will be over, because people will always have their doubts. I can't do it."

"Think about this, Jack. Because, once you cross the line, you can't go back."

"I can't go to the police. I can't fucking do it."

"Do you realize what you're saying?"

"Yes."

"Then, you need to go back and cover your tracks, as if you were never there, as if you never met Delilah. That's what you must do, and do it tonight. Time's running out."

"Charlie. I have to find Charlie."

My jaw muscles hurt from clenching them. I wondered of Charlie's whereabouts and of our friendship and of his loyalty. The camcorder rubbed against my ribs with each step. I fought the urge to view the tape, knowing there would be a better time for that once I found Charlie. Maybe, the tape held my alibi, and maybe, it didn't. I walked three more blocks to a phone booth and searched my pockets for change, but all I found was the cocktail napkin with Charlie's new telephone number scribbled on it and the phone card he gave me hours earlier.

After six rings, Charlie's answering machine picked up. When the beep finally came, I said, "Charlie, pick up the phone, man. It's Jack. Where are you? If you're there, pick up your goddamn phone. I'm in trouble. I'm walking around out here. I don't know where the hell I am. I'm by a church. Can't see the name. I'm on, wait a minute; I'm on the corner of—" And, that's when I was disconnected.

I dialed the 1-800 number again, entered the phone card's numbers, then Charlie's number, then waited. The female, computerized voice told me that my call could not be connected and to try again. I entered all the numbers again and waited, only to discover that the phone card no longer had any available minutes on it. In disbelief, I dialed again, and again the female, robot voice said, "You have no more minutes left. Goodbye." I slammed the receiver into its cradle and left the phone booth.

I walked another four blocks before ducking behind a row of bushes to take a piss. As my urine splashed on the ground, I heard something rustle about in the darkness. "Hey, man, what the fuck are you doing? This is my spot, man. Stop pissing on my spot, asshole. I'm sleeping here, son of a bitch," the raspy, drunken voice demanded. I jumped from behind the bushes and tripped onto the sidewalk. My penis scraped on the concrete when I fell, but the camcorder stayed secure in my jacket, under my arm.

The homeless man's bellowing laughter subsided into a wheezing fit, then into a hacking cough and, knowing that he had surprised me more than I did him, made him crawl out from his sleeping bag for a better look. "I haven't seen anything that funny since I caught my buddy jacking off to a grocery store ad. He loved the feel of warm, honey-glazed hams. The big ones, the ones they sell around Christmas time, you know the ones. But, I think you might have got him beat, shithead. That's what you get for trying to piss on me."

"I wasn't trying. I didn't even know you were there, okay?," I admitted, standing and buttoning my fly.

"Don't try to be cute with me. Everybody knows this is my place, shithead. I'm Trashcan Dan-the man. I'm known around here, shit-for-brains. Ask anybody, they'll tell you. This is where I sleep, right where you pissed," he said, squinting his eyes at me.

"Sorry, man, um, do you know where—"

"It's safer right here than the park, a whole lot safer," he said, then rumbled up some phlegm and spat.

"Where are we, exactly, like where are we at?"

"I ain't going to help you. Why should I? You pissed all over my shit, shithead," he said with widened eyes.

"I know, I know, and I'm sorry, okay, Trashcan Sam, but I really need—"

"Hey! You deaf? It's Trashcan Dan, not Sam. Get it right. Shit, man, you can't learn nothing perfect, can you, shit-for-brains? Only a weak son-of-a-bitch says 'Trashcan Sam.' Are you trying to be a funny son-of-a-bitch? Well, are you or not, huh, shithead?"

He eyeballed me with great intensity, and I believed he wanted to hear a yes to his question.

"No, not at all. Look, I just need to get to a nightclub called Mariposa Oscura, okay? That's it. Do you know of it? I'll leave right now."

"Nah, don't know of any place called that... but I do know where... wait, oh, wait, are you talking about that place where all them weird folks go, all dressed in women's panties and such, looking like circus freaks, wearing all that leather and crazy shit like that?"

"Yeah, yeah, circus freaks, right. Has three levels. You know of it?"

"Let me see... I think it might be— nope, I don't know of any place like that, can't help you. Now, get the hell out of here, shithead. Can't you see I was sleeping?"

"Hey, man, I'm in a fucked up situation right now, and I really need you to tell where that place is, like right now, okay? I need some help."

"You got wax in your ears, shit-for-brains? I told you to get the hell out of here. You're getting on my nerves, and so is your ugly face. You look like a pair of dirty socks. Now, go on.

Take off," he said and took a step closer.

"Okay, okay, what if I give you something for your time and information? I have a new phone card and this here ring. It's real silver. See?"

"Silver, huh? I do like real silver, always have. Let me see that ring and that phone card before I change my mind."

When I handed him the items, he examined both sides of the phone card, tucked it into his back pocket, and asked, "How many minutes does it have on it?," then licked his smallest finger on his left hand and forced the ring onto it.

"I think, like, 20, maybe, 30, but I'm not sure. Now, do we have a deal? The ring fits, looks good on you."

He gazed at the ring for a moment, rotating his hand, trying to catch enough light to make it shine.

"It does look good on my finger, doesn't it? Yes, sir, it does. Makes me look sophisticated, like I got brains, like I'm a somebody."

"Where's the Mariposa Oscura, Trashcan Dan?"

"I'm starting to recall that place. Yes, it's coming to me; oh, here it comes; okay, got it. You go three blocks that way, then there's a parking lot, but don't turn there, keep walking for another block. Then you're going to see a liquor store, used to be Bennie's, but I can't remember the new guy's name. He's an asshole, doesn't believe in credit. Anyway, it's next to a Chinese restaurant with red letters; that's where you take a left and go another two blocks. That's the way," he said and lumbered away toward his sleeping bag.

"Where is it?," I asked, stepping forward.

"On the corner, you'll see it, shit-for-brains. Now, leave me alone."

I watched him return and disappear behind the row of bushes, as though he was never there; and, as I began walking away, I recited Trashcan Dan's directions, so not to lose the information. "What if he gave me the wrong directions? What if that crazy bastard's laughing to himself right now? I could be wandering about all night," I thought. I kept walking, fading away into the night, before shouting, "Thanks a lot, Trashcan Dan, you, son-of-a-bitch.   Thanks a lot, shithead."

CHAPTER 18

It didn't take long to find that liquor store and Chinese restaurant with the red letters and, just like the homeless guy said, after taking a left, the Mariposa Oscura stood two blocks in the distance, right on the corner, right where I had left it. I was thrilled to discover that Trashcan Dan wasn't such a shithead after all. He actually gave me the God honest truth, and I kind of felt bad about the phone card, but I had bigger things to worry about, like trying to locate Charlie.

I knew the odds of finding Charlie were against me, but that didn't shake my determination. I had to try, right? So, I kept walking toward the crowd of people lingering about on the next block. I could've sworn I saw Charlie more than a few times in the crowd; I believe I even heard his voice call my name, but I knew it was only my imagination playing tricks on me.

As I stood on the corner waiting for the light to change, I watched strangers on the next block having fun, laughing with each other, and carrying on as most drunk people do on Saturday nights. Most of the drivers that passed me sped through the streets with purpose, while others cruised looking for company. A sedan filled with rowdy teenagers drove by, and one of the boys leaned out of the rear window and tried spitting on me. I closed my eyes and turned my back toward the fading laughter; I hoped that little son-of-a-bitch had lousy aim and believed that he did.

When the traffic light turned green and I proceeded to cross the street, my vision blurred; and again, I swallowed the bitter taste of cocaine. Every sound garbled, as if, at that moment, the entire city shouted into my ears in anger; and in a flash, I returned to Delilah: her green eyes, so soft, so full of life, and her sultry voice asking if I found her beautiful. There she was again, in my mind, swaying her body in front of me, asking for reassurance, but her words carried no sound. They were hollow, as though I had lost my hearing. When response was given, I watched her ask again; but this time, my imagination played a terrible trick and replaced her words with "Why didn't you save me?" The thought replayed once more before I was nearly struck by a speeding vehicle. The truck's screeching tires captured my attention, and its blinding headlights prevented me from seeing the driver. "You stupid motherfucker! Are you trying to get yourself killed?," the driver shouted. I stood frozen, mouth agape, without response, because it sounded, as though Charlie was speaking to me. "Well, just don't stand there with your thumb up your ass. Get in, Jack, we're holding up traffic," Charlie yelled. I hurried to the passenger side and jumped into the truck. Charlie sped into traffic, smelling of booze and cigarettes.

"You should've seen your face, Jacky. You looked like you shit your pants, dude," Charlie said, laughing, as he pulled the last drag from his smoke. "I looked all over the place for you. Where did you run off to? Tell me you left with a chick, dude, because that's the only reason I'll accept. You're lucky I found you. I was going to circle around one more time and—"

"Charlie?"

"Man, you missed out. I hooked up with this blonde in pink latex. Did you see her? She has a huge geisha tattoo on her back, so fucking sexy, dude. Gave me her phone number, motherfucker. I started grinding on her on the dance floor, you know what I mean, right? Bang, bang, bang! Just like that, and she fucking loved it. I swear it, no fucking lie, dude. That's the balls, right?"

"Yeah."

"Yeah? That's it? What the hell, Jack? I tell you about this blond, hot piece of ass in a pink, latex bodysuit, and all you got to say is 'Yeah.' I'm trying to tell you—"

"Charlie, I'm fucking scared, dude. I don't know...."

"Wait, you're what? What are you talking about, Jack? Are you serious right now, really?"

"I'm in trouble, serious trouble. I fucked up bad. I can't go to prison. She stole the cash, then we were in this taxi, and he wouldn't stop, and she kept saying fun and mystery, fuck, and—"

"Who stole what cash? Slow down. What?"

"I followed her. 'Fun and mystery,' she kept saying. I don't even know what that fucking means. She was taping us, and they killed her. They killed her. Oh, my God."

I turned away from Charlie and began weeping, pressing my face into the door's cold, metal frame; and again, I was drifting somewhere in outer space, cold, alone, and weightless, spinning into complete darkness. Charlie gripped my shoulder and told me to stop crying, as an older brother would. His animated tone had shifted to one of serious concern.

Charlie swiveled his head and eyed me, realizing something grave was at hand, and then returned his sights to the road. "What exactly are we talking about here, Jack? What kind of shit are you in right now?," he asked, lighting the end of his cigarette.

I composed myself and explained the situation to the best of my ability, from the beginning to the present, running down all the details. When Charlie asked to view the camcorder's contents, I rewound the tape and pressed the "play" button. Delilah had recorded, almost in a documenting fashion, some of her sexual exploits. It appeared that she had little to no sexual inhibitions. She enjoyed having rough sex and all sorts of bondage with men and women, sometimes, at the same time. What seemed unusual about her recordings wasn't the subject matter, but rather that they appeared clandestine, as though she was the only person in the room who was privy to the camcorder. The recordings were all conducted in her apartment, all from the same camera position, and the middle-aged man from the Polaroids kept appearing on the tape, but in various scenes.

The tape's timestamp indicated that the last recording with this man was approximately a week before her murder. It appeared that this man was, perhaps, a client of hers, because they often repeated the same sexual routine. Delilah, as his dominatrix, would bind him in restraints, walk about the room while humiliating him, and this was only the beginning of their ritual. She also whipped, sodomized, and paraded him about the room by a dog leash before golden showering him. By the looks of it, she seemed to enjoy her work, because, at times, she played to the camera, as though it was her private audience, flirting with the camera's eye.

However, it was hard to tell if this man knew about the camcorder, because he didn't stare directly into the camera's lens, like Delilah, but he did face the camera. This white, middle-aged, well-groomed man appeared wealthy and greatly experienced with the S&M lifestyle and its practices. And, as oddly as it seemed, the man appeared familiar to me. I imagined him to be the type of person who owns a closet filled with custom-tailored suits, married to a trophy wife, and possesses more than his share of country club memberships.

Charlie remained quiet as he stole glimpses of the recordings. I could tell that his mind was hard at work, on what exactly, I didn't know. He smoked his cigarette in silence, except for mumbling a few words to himself. When the videotape ended and the LCD screen turned blue, Charlie asked, "Is that it? There has to be more tape, Jack. That can't be it." I examined the camcorder's functions and pressed the "rewind," "stop" and "play" buttons several times.

"Don't break the goddamn thing. What the hell did you do?," Charlie asked.

My arms went limped in disbelief, causing the camcorder to fall onto the truck's floorboard. "I didn't do anything. It's the tape. The tape ran out," I said, then picked up the camcorder and rewound the tape again.

"See? That's me, right there; do you see that? I'm sitting down next to her; we're kissing and making out, and then I walk into her bedroom, right before they show up. But, you can't see that part, because the fucking tape ran out. That's what I'm trying to tell you. The fucking tape ran out. This isn't going to help me. It doesn't show who murdered her. Do you understand now? The tape ran out, Charlie. Where are we going? Where the hell are you taking me, man?"

Charlie remained silent and finished his cigarette, then offered me one, which I accepted without thought. "Why are you looking at me like that? No, you don't— you don't think I had anything to do with her murder, do you? You fucking better not, tell me you don't. I need to hear it, Charlie. Let me hear you say it."

"If you want me to help you, Jack, you're going to have to do everything I say, which means no questions, not even why I'm helping you. If you agree, then we'll start by sweeping your tracks. Otherwise, it's only a matter of time before the police find you. It's up to you; it's your choice, but you better make it fast, because you're running out of time," Charlie said, pulled the final drag from his cigarette and flicked it out of the window.

"Okay."

"Okay, what? This isn't some fucking game, Jack. If we do this shit, it isn't going to matter if you murdered her or not, because in the eye of the law, you did. Why else would you want to make her disappear? Do you understand what I'm telling you?"

"Yes. I do. I understand."

"Okay, then. Let's get you out of this trap."

When we arrived at Charlie's apartment, Charlie went into his bedroom and produced a black duffle bag, the kind with wheels on one end and a handle on the other. He began tossing items into the bag; at the time, they seemed randomly chosen, but later, I discovered each item had its essential purpose in the plan. Old towels, beanie caps, dish washing gloves, long-sleeved shirts; pairs of these went into the duffle, except for the large, kitchen knife and roll of duct tape. The sight of the knife caused my stomach to churn and send me to the toilet.

While I stood at the sink washing my hands, I stared into the eyes of a familiar stranger, watching his glassy pupils dilate in to a greater space of black. I turned away from the reflection in the mirror and felt my skin crawl, as though invisible bugs ran up my arms and chest, over my shoulders, and down my back. I shook them off, turned off the light, and walked out of the restroom.

I saw Charlie snort two lines of cocaine off of his cheap, white and gold-speckled, formica kitchen countertop. He tilted back his head and snorted into the air to help the coke drain better. And while he did this, he motioned for me to snort the other two lines that were waiting for me. And, there we were: Charlie and I, standing in his sorry-looking kitchen, snorting into the air, like two animals trying to catch a scent, and swallowing the bitter taste of cocaine down our throats. "The bag's ready," he said, nodding at the zipped duffle, then cleaned the counter with a single swipe of his hand. "Ain't got much time now."

With the duffle in the truck bed, we drove toward the Mariposa Oscura again. Charlie spoke on what needed to be done and how we were going to do it. I couldn't believe what I was hearing, because Charlie's plan to dispose of the body sounded too simple to actually work, but I didn't say anything about it. I just listened. He said that we were to refrain from using her name, and I agreed; and when he asked the whereabouts of Delilah's apartment, I repeated the homeless guy's directions and attempted to place them in the reverse order, but found it too confusing. It didn't matter, though, because Charlie knew his way around the city and said that we would backtrack from the nightclub.

Charlie continued speaking of the plan and used unfamiliar words, such as colectomy, gastrectomy, forensic evidence, gas bacillus, gastric incisions, postmortem bleeding, and some others. He then attempted to explain hydrodynamics, hydro-erosion, and their relation to gravity. It was all too much for me to comprehend and brought feelings of ineptitude, insecurity, confidence, and, overall, blind faith.

When I questioned Charlie on how he knew of all these things, he said, "Learned most of it from Mr. Splakovic, junior and senior year. I kinda learned the other shit from the television and a couple of books, but, mostly, from cable and PBS. I fucking love PBS, dude. They got some quality shit going on…."

Again, I nodded in agreement, remembering that Charlie had worked as an assistant for our high school, science teacher Mr. Splakovic. I tried convincing myself that everything was going to be fine. That everything was going to work according to the plan. I mean, what other option did I have? Besides, I thought Charlie sounded like a goddamn scientist, like he actually knew what he was doing. I, on the other hand, had no fucking clue what hydrodynamics, gastrectomy, gas bacillus, and some of the other words meant, but I knew I wasn't alone in this anymore, and that's what mattered the most to me.

CHAPTER 19

Driving by the Mariposa Oscura, the surrounding area and streets began to seem familiar, and it didn't take us long to find Delilah's street and apartment building. We found a shadowed parking space across the street from the brownstone building and wedged the truck in between a white BMW and silver Benz sedan. No one knew that there was a lumped-over, dead body in the living room of a fourth floor apartment, no one but Charlie and I, the two murderers, and the person who commissioned the murder, so we hoped. Charlie advised that we act as though we were visiting a friend and nothing more. "I'll get the bag, " he said and stepped out of the truck, then craned his neck over his shoulder and whispered, "Just act normal, and everything will be fine, trust me. Come on."

The building's small lobby was empty, smelled of fading perfume and stale cigarette smoke, and the only sound heard was our rubber soles on the tile floor. The moment we entered the elevator and Charlie pressed the fourth floor button, my hands became clammy, and I wiped my palms on my pants. The doors closed and held our reflections in its polished, stainless steel. Charlie eyed me hard, produced a half-smile, and handed me two, plastic grocery bags. I accepted them without question and tucked them into my pocket. The creaking sounds of the elevator's mechanical moving parts found their way inside and kept us company as we ascended. "They're for our feet. We'll bag them, tape them, so there's less evidence. First thing, okay?, he said." I nodded as the elevators doors opened, and we stepped out into the calm hallway. The fragrance of fresh-cut flowers lingered in the air and smelled of lilac, eucalyptus, and some other scent that was unrecognizable to me. More than ever in my life, I wished to be in any other place than where I was, leading Charlie to a dead woman's apartment. And, as if Charlie knew my thoughts, he whispered, "Don't worry; we'll be out of here in five minutes, ten at most."

I walked passed three more doors and stopped at the fourth and said, "This is where she lives," then looked up and down the hallway, anticipating a neighbor to open his door and see us standing there looking suspicious.

"Are you sure this is the right door? If you have any doubt, tell me now. Is this the right door, Jack?"

"This is the one. But, I don't remember locking it. I could've, but I don't remember. I'm not sure."

"Not sure if it's locked or if it's the right apartment?"

"If it's locked."

Charlie handed me the duffle, placed the bottom end of his shirt around the doorknob, and opened Delilah's door. We entered the apartment, closed and locked the door. Everything appeared as how I had left it, except for the porno movie on the television. The movie had ended and the T.V. screen was now blue. Charlie stared at the dead body for a moment before unzipping the duffle bag. Without a word, we encased our feet in plastic, grocery bags, put on the long-sleeved shirts, hid our hair beneath the beanie caps, and pulled on the gloves. The plan had officially commenced.

We moved the sofa and coffee table away from the bearskin rug, giving us more space to work. Delilah had hidden the camcorder's remote control under the sofa, perhaps, when I showered. "I've never seen anything like this. She looks like Nicole Kidman, except for her hair. This is some real crazy shit, man. I need for you put everything back, like you never touched it, and put her clothes in the bathroom," Charlie ordered. "Make sure you wipe your prints off of everything. Take the towels, and remember what I told you, swift and precise. Now, get to it. Time's ticking away."

In the bedroom, I gathered the pile of clothes that I used as camouflage and returned them to their rack, wiping my fingerprints as I backtracked my actions. I then moved the pillow and found the sex toys and lotion bottle and returned them to the trunk, but not before placing the stack of Polaroids in my pocket. I closed the lid and made sure that all of my prints were wiped clean from each item that I touched earlier in the evening. All traces that I had entered Delilah's bedroom were now gone.

When I entered the living room, Charlie had already laid Delilah on her back and folded both of her arms. The palms of her hands rested on her shoulders, and Charlie was in the process of wrapping duct tape around her upper torso, just below her shoulder joints. The gruesome sight was paralyzing, and it entered my eyes with the velocity and precision of a marksman's kill shot. He continued folding and duct taping Delilah's legs in the same fashion as her arms, reducing her size with each movement, folding and taping at all of her major joints, as though she was nothing more than a piece of folding furniture. For the first time, I feared Charlie. He worked with the efficiency of an experienced game hunter. Swift and precise. He looked at me with sweat building on his brow and said, "Shit, man, just don't stand there. I can't do this alone. I need your help. We need to make her small enough to fit into the duffle bag. Now, Jack."

Delilah's dead and twisted body sickened me to the point of nearly vomiting. I turned away and covered my mouth. "Now, Jack!," I heard again. I closed my eyes, felt saliva building in my mouth, and then my stomach convulsed and erupted. However, I remembered that bile holds DNA, so I tightened my mouth and swallowed hard and kept swallowing until it was all gone. When the acids bubbled up and burned the back of my throat, I coughed and gagged into the crook of my arm, leaving me with watery eyes and gasping for air. "We're not going to get a second chance at this. I need your help, man," Charlie said. "Fucking hurry up." His narrowed eyes were full of determination, and he wasn't going to allow me to turn cowardice on the situation. I approached and waited for direction.

"Get yourself together; this shit isn't easy for me either. We just have to get through it, okay? Now, I'm going to lift her up, and you're going to wrap that tape around her arms and tits, you got it? Ready. Go," Charlie said, then lifted Delilah's torso upright off of the floor. "What the hell are you waiting for, start wrapping her up. Don't worry, you're not going to hurt her, trust me. She's not going to feel a thing."

As I circled the roll of duct tape around her biceps and breasts, transferring the roll from one hand to another, Charlie said, "Faster, Jack, come on."

"Is that good enough?"

"Not yet, keep going."

I circled her body two more times before Charlie said, "Okay, that'll work. It looks about right, but we need to fold both of her legs so her knees are touching her tits. You know what I'm saying?"

"Let's do what we have to do and get the hell out of here. And, for God's sake, Charlie, can you please close her fucking eyes. She's staring right at me. Jesus," I said, looking away from her.

"Relax, we're almost done. Grab her legs and be careful…."

After more forceful folding and twisting and duct taping of her limbs, Delilah's body was compact enough to place her inside the black bag, but not entirely. We had placed her facing upward, but discovered that she wasn't going to fit as expected. It wasn't her body that was the problem; it was her head. It stuck out of one end of the bag. Charlie repositioned the body, but he was still unable to make her head fit into the bag, and this began to frustrate him. He cursed under his breath and pushed and pushed on her head, trying to get it below the zipper, until we heard the unmistakable sound of a cracked bone. Charlie had pushed so hard on Delilah's head that he broke her neck, causing it to rest abnormally askew.

"Oh, fuck, dude. Oh, my God, that's—"

"Shut up. It's not like I did it on purpose. I guarantee she didn't feel it, so stop worrying about her so much. She's fucking dead, Jack, but how do you think I feel? It's not like I do this kind of shit everyday, and don't forget why were here, okay?"

He then told me to get the bearskin rug and roll it nice and tight and stuff it into the bag. "Hurry up, we're almost done," he said, wiping his sweaty forehead onto his sleeve. And like a robot, I did exactly what Charlie instructed and watched as he conducted the final sweep of the apartment. He moved about the place, turning off the VCR, stereo, television, and then slid the sofa and coffee table back to their proper places, again wiping down every item he touched. He picked up the broken, glass pieces from the kitchen floor and tossed them into the trash and then scooped up most of the fallen soil. Charlie appeared methodical in his thoughts and movements and questioned if the apartment appeared as it did some hours ago.

After answering his question, he said,

"Okay, now, take off your gloves and put them in the bag and don't touch a single thing with your bare hands, not one thing." Our gloves went into the bag and, as Charlie did some minutes earlier, I, too, used the bottom of my shirt to wrap around the doorknob. "Peek out first and don't forget the bags, Jack," he said. "We can't be seen walking out of here with bags on our feet." I opened the door and discovered an empty hallway. "Let's go while we still have a chance," I whispered, tearing the plastic from my feet and handing it to Charlie. He tucked them into the black bag, secured the zipper, and closed the apartment door on his way out into the hallway. The black bag appeared solid and heavy, but it rolled down the hallway and into the elevator with ease.

When we reached the lobby and the elevator doors opened, we exited Delilah's apartment building and headed straight for Charlie's truck. Charlie placed the bag into the uncovered truck bed and stepped in to the driver's seat, as though the black bag was nothing more than what it was. A black duffle bag.

CHAPTER 20

Police sirens wailed in the near distance, and we drove away from the brownstone building. I couldn't tell if it was the cocaine or the adrenaline, but something surged within me, some sort of electric energy coursed through my veins, and I knew the feeling would soon be out of my control. Charlie didn't say much as he drove through the city streets. He smoked his cigarette in a relaxed manner, almost too relaxed for my liking. Then, I saw something wash over him, not entirely, but enough for me to know that his thoughts were now in some far off distant place. He looked emotionally numb and physically exhausted, and I assumed that, even though it pains me to admit, a part of Charlie also died in that apartment. And knowing that he cared enough to put himself in harm's way for me, for our friendship, made something also die within me. These pieces of ourselves could never be restored, no matter how hard or long we tried.

Charlie tossed his pack of cigarettes on my lap, then his lighter, and said, "Don't worry, Jacky; everything's going to be just fine. You just wait and see." I believed his words more than ever this time, but whether he believed them was a different story. "Everything's going to be just fine," he repeated and looked at me. Charlie drove the speed limit, stopped at all the stops signs, used his blinkers for each turn and lane change, and often looked in the rearview mirror, but never appeared nervous.

The hilly streets of the city caused the bag to slide around in the truck bed; and more than a couple of times, when Charlie braked or accelerated, the bag would change direction, sliding forward toward the cab, then backward toward the tailgate, and forward again. I hummed whatever tune entered my mind to block out that repeating thud, but it didn't help at all, and I imagined that it was Delilah, herself, pounding on the truck in anger, but I knew better, so I hummed louder, reached for another cigarette, and grimaced each time that horrific sound came. On the following block, that's when it happened: a police car appeared in Charlie's rearview mirror.

"Stay calm," Charlie said. I agreed, but my heart didn't, and it raced and pounded, but not as before. The rhythm felt odd. My heart pumped normally for a series of beats, then it would pause for a beat, and then beat so greatly that my chest felt deep and heavy. I feigned calm while spotting the police car in Charlie's side mirror. There was a foreboding presence about it, the way it appeared out of nowhere and slowly followed a car-length behind us, as though it had been waiting since the very moment we drove away from Delilah's apartment.

"You think he's running your plates? He's going to pull us over, isn't he?," I asked, wiping my clammy hands on my pants.

"He isn't going to do shit. He's patrolling the neighborhood, probably thinks I'm drunk. And, yeah, he's definitely running my plates. He's looking for any reason to stop us, but stay calm and get your shit together, Jack. Don't panic, alright?"

"Yeah. I'm not. I'm so fucking chill right now, dude. I'm calm, so fucking calm. See?," I said, showing Charlie my trembling hands.

"Yeah, whatever, just keep it together. When he pulls us over, let me do all the talking, okay? Deep breaths and don't let the cops see that."

"Yes," I said, then filled my lungs with air and exhaled.

Charlie checked his speed, remained steady, and mumbled that he should've checked his taillights.

"Why is he still following us?," I asked, feeling my heartbeat in my ears.

"It'll be routine, quick and easy," Charlie said, with his eyes stuck in his rearview mirror.

At that moment, the red and blue lights were set in motion and the siren chirped. "Here, we go," Charlie said and clicked on his turn signal and began pulling to the side of the residential street. "If he asks you where we're going, tell him we're on a date."

"We're on a what?"

"A date, just do it. We met at the Mariposa Oscura and I was taking you home, okay? That's what we did. We're on a date. Don't say another word."

The police car parked behind us and turned his spotlight on us; and within a minute, the police officer stood at the driver side window and had Charlie's driver's license in hand. He asked Charlie if he had used drugs or alcohol this evening and if he was aware that one of his taillights was out. Each one of the police officer's questions was standard, but as he handed back Charlie's license, he asked, "What's in the back?"

"Clothes. My boyfriend's dirty clothes," Charlie said and placed his right hand on my inner thigh and kept it there. The officer lowered his sights, saw Charlie's hand stoking my thigh, and appeared slightly disgusted.

"Have a good night and get that taillight fixed," the officer said and walked back to his patrol car, turned off the lights, and sped away.

"Wholly shit, dude. I can't even— Oh, my God, what the fuck just happened?"

"Nothing. Nothing happened. That's what happened," Charlie said, started his truck, clicked on his turn signal, and pulled away from the curb.

I rolled down the window, craned out my head, and vomited while Charlie drove into the night.

We soon drove into a near-empty parking lot by the marina and found a space to park. Charlie turned off the headlights and killed the engine. "Hey, I need to ask you something before we do this," Charlie said, shooting me with a deadpan stare. "Faith. Do you believe in it?"

"Yeah, I need get out of this truck, though. I need fresh air, feeling kind of dizzy," I said, beginning to open the door.

"Wait!," Charlie said, as he gripped my shoulder. "There's no turning back from this, Jack— ever. And, I need to know if you really do have faith. No bullshit. Don't you understand? Because, that's all we have to go on and all we'll ever have. Look, it's like we're about to go up against a world of shit and we have to believe that we're going to end up on top. Nothing's guaranteed. You realize what I'm saying, right?"

"Yeah, and I do have faith, Charlie. If I didn't, I wouldn't be here," I said, opening the door.

"That's what I needed to hear. 'Cause, we're going to need it. Now, help me with the bag, and don't forget the camcorder."

When we stepped out of the truck, Charlie pointed to a pile of landscaping stones, which rested near some bushes and an unfinished landscaping project. "We need a few of those, maybe, four or five. That should be plenty."

CHAPTER 21

The sound of ocean waves crashing on the shore rose above all other city sounds; and in the nearby distance, the lights from the Palace of Fine Arts sliced into the darkness. Alcatraz, Coit Tower, Bay Bridge, Golden Gate Bridge, and more could be seen with a quick spin of the feet. On any other given night, these landmarks would've been nothing less than breathtaking, but there was something ominous in the air that robbed them of their beauty.

Upon reaching the pile of stones, I rested down on my haunches and collected as much as I could carry. Some 35 feet away, Charlie rolled the black bag to the harbor's gated entrance and waited; and more than a couple of times, I doubted that I could carry an arm full of landscaping rocks to the entrance, but I did it without dropping a single stone. A gust of wind blew into the bay and salt was tasted upon my lips. There was something about the crisp, ocean air that reduced my anxiety and refreshed my clarity; and now, I sincerely believed that the plan could actually work, but the most challenging part was still to be seen.

Some 600 yards away, a thick fog layer began entering the bay and blanketing the highest points of the Golden Gate Bridge. Charlie rolled the bag behind him, and I followed, and the rubber wheels rolled over each of the dock's wooden boards. Charlie soon stopped between two boats and said, "This it is. Hand me those rocks," and stepped aboard one of the boats. It was a light-green boat, some 30 or so feet in length and extremely used. As I handed Charlie the five rocks, I remembered how he would talk about fishing with his stepdad on the bay, but he hadn't mentioned fishing or his stepfather in a long time, as least, not in the way he would speak of them years ago. "Give me the bag, but be careful. It's heavier than it looks," he said, leaning over with open arms. "Now, release the mooring lines."

Charlie knew I hadn't the slightest clue of what he had just said. "Untie the ropes and get in, Jack," he said, making his way to the boat's cockpit. He started the engine, creating movement within the black water, and moved about the boat, checking this, checking that, and the other. From where I was sitting, it looked like Charlie knew what he was doing, and I felt more secure in his boating abilities, but not so confident in the boat itself. "Everything checks out. We're good to go," Charlie said, sitting down in the captain's chair and steering the boat out of the marina.

When we approached the jetty and faced Alcatraz Island, Charlie told me to bring two lifejackets from the cabin; and as I stepped below the deck, I wondered how far Charlie was planning to take us. I searched the cabinets and pulled out two, orange lifejackets. They were old, frayed around the edges, and smelled tangy, like stale, vinegary fish, but it made no difference. I followed my orders and brought them to Charlie. When we were out of the marina, just beyond the buoys and heading toward the Golden Gate Bridge, Charlie repositioned the throttle and brought the boat to a moderate cruising speed. The engine growled, deep and steady, and the boat's hull plowed through the rough waters without a struggle. Several white birds flew overhead and disappeared into the night sky, and the wind pushed into us, whispering into our ears. The glowing skyline, with all of its radiating lights, grew faint in the distance, but the Golden Gate Bridge, larger than ever, shined bright against the black background and created the illusion that the ocean no longer existed beyond its structure; and its rows of pale-white lights, the ones that stretch from one end to the next, reminded me of lustrous pearls strung along a woman's necklace. I wished to be in some other place, anywhere than where I was.

The oncoming waves slapped the hull and salty mist sprayed up from both sides of the boat. Charlie reassured that we had enough gas for the round trip, and that everything would be fine. But even with Charlie's words, I remained silent with dreadful thoughts of capsizing and drowning in the black, white-capped waters. Again, I saw that painting from the Mariposa Oscura, the one that held the indelible images of an old man and a centaur in a small, wooden rowboat adrift in a blood-red sea, surrounded by hundreds of drowning men and women, all flailing, all moments away from their death.

Scenes from Delilah's apartment raided my mind and appeared like grainy snapshots taken with a disposable camera: the moment Delilah leaned over and kissed me on the lips and slowly moved her hands over her moist body; discovering her Polaroids in her trunk of sex paraphernalia; photographs of Delilah dressed as a dominatrix, her green eyes staring out from behind a black, leather mask; nude men and women in bondage, all bent, strapped, and bound in ecstasy. I freed my mind of the disturbing images, but the scent of fresh-cut lilac and eucalyptus entered my nose, as though I held them in my hand, as though I was once again in that infamous hallway. Delilah's haunting laugh began echoing in my head so loudly that I had no other choice but to look at the black bag. I imagined that she was kicking and punching and screaming to get out.

I reached into my right, front pocket and removed the Polaroids and began flipping though them. I then noticed that the same man who appeared in most of the photographs, the one who seemed strangely familiar, had an identifying mark on his right buttock, a coat of arms hovering above three letters. At first, I assumed he received the tattoo from his fraternity as a sign of passage, but as I took a closer look at the other pictures, specifically the group pictures, I noticed the same tattoo and placement on a few other men and several women. This marking was not from a college fraternity, but a fraternity of some other kind. I then wondered if I had actually seen this man before or if he merely had one of those familiar types of faces, as some people do. Delilah's death, the photographs, the same familiar man in the pictures and video recordings, and the rest were all too confusing for me at the moment. Quite honestly, I had no clue of what to make of them, but I suspected they were connected in some way, directly or indirectly; they had to be.

I stuffed the pictures back into my pocket as we boated underneath the Golden Gate Bridge and out to deeper and rougher waters. Raising his voice above the engine, Charlie yelled, "Bring me a spool of fishing line, the thickest line you could find and a couple of large fishing hooks." He pointed in the direction of the needed items. "Then bring the chum. It's in a white bucket in the refrigerator. There should be enough in there."

Everything was easily found, but the white bucket weighed lighter than I expected, only one-third of it was filled and smelled of stale fish blood. When I brought this to Charlie's attention, he replied, "It's not a problem; because where we're headed, that's plenty. They'll smell that blood in the water and they'll come hungry. They'll take all of her... and if they don't, hydro-erosion will, you know what I mean?"

The black swells grew and caused the boat to rise and fall and rise again. "Hold on," Charlie shouted, as he tightened his grip on the wheel. "Hold on, Jack. It's going to get rough. We're—" An oncoming wave violently slapped the boat and silenced Charlie's speech. As I held on, Charlie fidgeted with the instrument panel and tightened the straps on his lifejacket. More water had entered the boat and splashed and onto the duffle bag, and the air felt colder than ever. We had traveled miles, but none were as treacherous as the ones being taken at that moment. If anything had happened to us, no one would have ever known. Vulnerability loomed everywhere. "We're headed toward the edge of the Red

Triangle, by the Farallon Islands," Charlie said, steering the boat out into the darkness.

"Let's do it here. We don't need to go any farther. Let's stop the boat and do it here. Fuck it, Charlie. This is as good a place as any other, right? Kill the engine," I yelled, leaning toward Charlie.

"Hell, no, not here. I know what I'm doing, and we need to go farther out, far enough so that the current doesn't wash her body back into the bay and onto shore. Don't worry, man. They're migrating, and there's tons of them right now."

"What's migrating?"

Charlie turned with a deadpan stare, as if deciding whether to speak or remain silent, so I asked again.

"Great Whites."

"Like sharks?"

"Yeah, like sharks. What else is there? They're migrating, probably swimming below us right now, probably all around us— big, fucking, great white sharks with big fucking teeth and the blackest eyes you'll ever see," Charlie said, then twisted his face into a knot and howled at the sky, as if a deranged spirit had possessed him.

"Kill the engine. Stop this fucking boat, Charlie. I mean it," I said, punching Charlie in the arm.

Charlie chuckled, until realizing his attempt at humor wasn't playing well with me.

"Look, Jack, we need them. Probably won't eat her whole, but, maybe, they'll chomp on her enough to scatter her. Or, maybe, they won't. Maybe, she'll fucking sink to the bottom. But, stay calm, Jacky, okay? We're almost done."

"Charlie, man, listen to me. There's no reason why we can't do it here and be done with the whole damn thing. I have a bad feeling about this— a really bad feeling, dude, just stop the boat here, and let's do it, okay?"

"There's nothing to worry about it, Jacky. Sorry, if I messed with your head, but I've been there before, and we'll circle back before you know it. If you want something to worry about, worry about the fog; it's getting thick. You have faith in us or not, you and me getting out of this shithole or you want me to turn this fucking boat around and to go to the police and hope they believe you had nothing to do with that girl's murder? If you do, tell me now, Jack, and I'll do it. I'll turn back right fucking now. But don't think for a minute that they're going to let you walk away into the sunset, like it's some goddamn movie, because they're not. What are you thinking? We're going to roll her into the police station and unpack her taped up body on a cop's desk and say we had nothing to do with it?

What? We found her like that, duct taped in to a ball and stuffed into a duffle bag, is that what you're thinking?"

Charlie narrowed his eyes as salty mist blew in to us. "I'm trying to save your ass. Can't you see that? I could've turned my back on you, Jack, but I didn't. So, what's it going to be?," he shouted.

"I just want to get this shit over with. How much farther?"

"Good. Go get the camcorder, remove the tape and drop them both into the water. Take the beanies, the shirts, and the other shit and soak them in the chum… didn't mean to fuck with your head…."

While following the plan, oncoming waves crashed harder against the boat as it labored in and out of the heavy swells and continued pushing into the wind, carrying us farther and farther out to sea. The temperature had now dropped beyond complaint, so we held on and stayed the course. Another three miles were taken before Charlie shouted again. It had now started raining, and we were soaked to our bones within minutes. The rain fell hard and fast and felt like gravel being thrown against our cold-bitten faces. Charlie shouted another set of orders, but I couldn't hear what he said, so I staggered toward him.

"Take the wheel and keep it as straight as

possible! I'll get everything ready. It's going to get real tricky here, but just stay on course," Charlie said, "You ready? Take the wheel."

When I placed my hands on the wheel, Charlie stepped out of the captain's chair and stood behind me for a moment.

"What do you want to me to do again?," I asked, over my shoulder.

"Keep the bow pointed in the same direction and don't panic and don't touch anything. We're almost done. And, whatever you do, Jacky, just keep your fucking hands on the wheel, okay?," Charlie said and scrambled away.

I steered the boat and checked on Charlie, as he methodically prepared Delilah for disposal. He unzipped the black duffle, removed the bearskin rug, then sank his hands deeper into the bag and lifted out Delilah's folded body. The roll of duct tape, kitchen knife, and the other items were placed on the deck, next to Delilah, then he unfolded the bearskin rug, but quickly returned to the cockpit and pushed me out of the way and began pushing buttons on the instrument panel, killing the boat's engine and lights before moving the throttle in to another position. "Follow me and do exactly as I tell you. We have to move fast; we don't want to be seen dumping a body overboard," he said, then returned to the body.

As the boat rose and fell in between swells,

we pulled on the rubber gloves, placed the body on the rug, and kneeled around it. "Take the knife and cut her legs loose, then her arms. Hurry… good… now, make an incision from her sternum to her navel," Charlie instructed, as rain poured down on us.

Her pale, nude body appeared ghostly in the evening light, and seeing her there, stretched out on the bearskin rug rendered me useless. I tried moving my limbs, but couldn't. I remained frozen in the ghastly nightmare that teetered on reality: I knew what Charlie and I were doing at that moment, but it felt odd, like I was in someone else's body, even though, it was my hand that held that knife.

"Jack!," Charlie shouted, until pulling me out of my bewilderment. "Insert the knife below her sternum and drag it down to her bellybutton, like you're gutting a deer. Don't look at her face. Drive it in and do it now, Jack! Now!"

"Let's just throw her over and get the hell out of here before we get caught. Fuck cutting her open, man. Fuck that shit. I can't do it. I can't."

"Give me the knife," Charlie demanded and grabbed the knife from my hand.

Without hesitation, Charlie drove the knife's point into Delilah's body, making the incision from her breasts to her navel in one swift movement. It was done, and her blood and intestines oozed out of the vertical opening.

"Take her guts out and throw them overboard. I'll cut them free. Just scoop them out. Don't think about it, just get in there with both hands and do it. Fucking do it, Jack," Charlie shouted. "Fucking do it!"

I shoved both of my hands into the opening and dug out her slimy guts with repulsion, scooping them out as if digging a hole into a muddy creek bed.

"That's it. Yeah, just like that, just like that, keep going, all of it... get all of it... good, man, good, you fucking lunatic, you crazy son-of-a-bitch," Charlie shouted, jabbing his fist into my shoulder, getting me to stop digging. "Okay, okay, now, get the rocks, the rocks, Jack. Hurry the fuck up, man, and bring the fishing line." As I lumbered to fetch the items, Charlie yelled something into the rain-drenched wind; what was said or to whom he was speaking, I'll never know, because his words were quickly swept away, as though they were never spoken.

Upon my return, Charlie began burying each stone inside her hollowed out belly and used a large fishing hook tied to heavy-gauge fishing line to stitch her back together. He looked across her body and said, "Don't just stand there. Fucking help me. Grab her legs. We're almost done." I bent down and wrapped my hands around her ankles, and Charlie lifted her torso. We then moved her toward the edge of the boat. "On three," Charlie said, staring at me unequivocally. "One. Two. Three!"

We lifted her over the edge of the boat and let go. Her pale body disappeared into the ocean's black and white-capped waves. She vanished from sight. Charlie sliced up our gloves and tossed them in the water along with all the other items, then emptied the chum bucket into the sea. Even though, we assumed that the rain had cleaned the deck of all blood, Charlie insisted that the deck be rinsed with a few buckets of water before he started the engine and shouted, "Hold on to something! We're getting the hell out of here, right fucking now!"

CHAPTER 22

Charlie turned the boat around toward the direction of the bay, and I made sure that every possible shred of evidence was thrown overboard. He kept shouting, "Everything must go into the ocean," over and over again. "If the Coast Guard stops us, don't say much; let me do all the talking. We're on our way back from fishing. That's all. Plain and simple. And, we didn't catch shit, got it? Lay some poles around. Make it look real. What did you do with the fishing line, the one I used to stitch her up?"

"It's gone, tossed it overboard," I said, securing the clasps on my lifejacket.

"Get rid of anything else. When this is over, we'll throw away our shoes in dumpsters somewhere along the peninsula, in different cities. Where's the bag? The bag," Charlie shouted, forcing his words through the rain.

Everything we had brought onto the boat some time ago now rested on the ocean's floor, somewhere within the Red Triangle's shark infested waters. We pushed through the hard rain and white-capped swells and felt the powerful sea move below us. Charlie navigated his boat into rolling swells and never appeared unnerved. I found strength in his unwavering courage. At times, with spray cresting over the bow, he would throttle forward and catch the next swell, momentarily melding with the ocean's ever-changing rhythm, then reposition the throttle and stare into the darkness. For the next several miles, we kept most of our thoughts to ourselves, hardly speaking a word to each other, and there was something calming yet equally unsettling about the silence.

When the rain softened, I pulled the photographs from my pocket and showed them to Charlie. His eyes widened with interest and disbelief, then reduced the boat's speed and told me to take the wheel. He remained silent as he inspected each Polaroid. Whenever I tried sharing my thoughts on a photo, he shushed me until he had seen the entire lot. He paused a moment, as if searching his mind for an answer, then surveyed me. "You found these in her apartment," he said, clearing rain from his eyes. "Are there any more?"

"I only found those, in her trunk, under all her sex toys and stuff. I think she tried hiding them. I know she did," I said.

"What makes you say that?"

"Because they were hidden. They weren't out in the open, like all of her other shit. They were tucked away in the joint of the trunk, in a corner, wedged into a tear in the lining. She made that pocket and hid them there. She had to, who else would've put them there? I don't know how I found them, but I did; and see that guy, he's on the videotape; he's all over it, and I've fucking seen that dude before. Don't ask me where, but I've seen that face. He looks familiar, doesn't he?"

Charlie handed me the photographs, sat behind the wheel, and said, "We should've kept the videotape, just in case— we really should've."

"You know who he is?"

"Yeah, me and a lot of other people. You know why he looks so familiar? It's because he's been on the fucking news for the last two weeks. He's Edward Salvador— the city councilman under investigation for taking bribes from building contractors and some other bullshit. Payoffs on the sly. Back alley deals, man. He makes money on the side and it's totally illegal, every single piece of it," Charlie said, then paused to stare at my puzzled expression.

"A councilman?"

"Hell, yeah, a councilman, more like a crook in a suit, man, but people like him. He's slick. You got to give him credit for that. He's sort of a small time celebrity around here, and he likes to fuck young interns, fresh out of college types. He almost got busted for that shit, too, but nothing came of it. He's scandalous," Charlie said with a smirk.

"Shit. I knew he looked familiar."

"Yeah, that's the guy, and that's why he had her killed. I wonder if it was his idea to make it look like a drug overdose, pretty fucking smart. Think about it, Jacky? Who really cares about some high-class whore overdosing on cocaine in her posh apartment? Do you know who cares?"

"Who?"

"Nobody. Nobody gives a shit about that, not here, anyway. It's just another statistic, maybe, not even that. But, I'll tell you what they do care about, what they really give a shit about—political vendettas and incriminating evidence, like those photographs, bet he didn't even know about the videotape or that you were hiding in the bedroom while his henchmen murdered his mistress. He had her killed, Jack. You see that, right? She could have ruined everything for him, destroyed him, and he knew it, and so—"

"He killed her."

"Exactly. If they had found you with her, there's a real good chance that you wouldn't be here right now. You'd be dead. Or, maybe, they would've made you their scapegoat and not think twice about it. Lock you up and throw away the key, know what I mean? Maybe, she knew her time was coming. I mean, why else would she secretly videotape him? Protection? Evidence? Who fucking knows why she taped anyone, right? Maybe, that was her thing. We'll never know, but, I'll tell you what. He wasn't going to allow her to publically humiliate him or his family and end his political career— not her, not some disposable whore…."

Charlie spoke so fast and continued stringing all the possible pieces together that it made me dizzy. I never could have imagined, not for a damn instant, that I would be involved in this grave ordeal, but there I was, in the middle of it all, and there was no denying it. Charlie rambled on; at times, it seemed as if he was talking to me, yet other times, it was as if he was talking to himself, and it didn't make much difference, not really, not anymore, but he just kept on talking, and hearing the sound of his voice, regardless of what he was saying, made me feel slightly better, because I knew I wasn't alone.

"You're lucky they didn't find you, Jack. Damn lucky," Charlie said, looking over at me.

"This is what it feels like, huh, Charlie?," I

asked, turning away in shame.

"We beat those guys, and they don't even know it yet. Checkmate, motherfuckers. Wholly shit, Jack! We won. You don't see that? I bet we couldn't do better if we tried; maybe, if we actually tried to beat them, we would've fucked it all up. I can almost guarantee it. The man upstairs was looking out for us, if you can believe it. Faith, Jack. Don't ever lose it."

"We won? Won, what exactly? Because, this feels so fucked up. It doesn't feel anything like winning, not how I remember it, so what are you talking about? What did we win?"

Charlie appeared amazed at his understanding of the situation that he chuckled and tapped the steering wheel with excitement, and I stood awkwardly clueless to the inside joke. He turned to me for a moment and asked with a smile, "What do you think those bastards are going to say when they find out her dead body's missing?" He laughed, reached out and gripped my shoulder, and his eyes gleamed with a renewed happiness.

"Jack, buddy, don't you get it? Haven't you figured it out yet? We're free and clear. Listen, they went through all that trouble to make Delilah's death look like an overdose, to make absolutely sure that she didn't have a chance to ruin Ed's public image, right? Shit, man, they left the fucking needle hanging out of her arm. But, here's the kick in the balls and the uppercut: they know they killed her, right? They know that for a fact, but where's her body? Where's the evidence? Where's her autopsy? Where's the fucking news report? A dead body just doesn't get up and walk out the door, Jack. Or, does it? Now, you following me? See, those bastards and that councilman will forever be wondering what happened to her, but they can't poke around for information, not if they want their plan to work. I mean, what are they going to say? Think for a minute. They're supposed to be completely clueless to Delilah. No ties to her and especially not to her murder, Jack. They're trapped in silence. We win— and, so, do they, in a fucked up kind of way."

"Yeah, I understand— everyone wins— everybody, except Delilah. Checkmate, right?"

Charlie remained quiet and steered his boat under the Golden Gate Bridge toward the marina; and in the distance, the city's lights glowed and twinkled with life, again reminding me of everyday people. I pulled out the photographs and flipped through them, thinking they should be kept for insurance purposes, just in case, but changed my mind and dropped them all overboard.

Upon returning to the first mate's chair, I looked at Charlie and attempted to read his mind, but it was pointless. What was done was done, and there wasn't anything in this world that could change it. Charlie's words echoed in my mind once more, and I realized we were all trapped in silence, every single one of us. Silently imprisoned within our own thoughts for the rest of our lives. At that moment, I knew I'd always wonder if Delilah was the true winner of this ordeal.

When we reached the marina and returned the boat to its slip, Charlie and I acted as if nothing had happened out there, nothing other than a night of fishing. We washed the deck once more, and no one suspected anything out of the ordinary. Nothing was ever reported to the police or the harbormaster. And, our secret, the one beyond everyday secrets, remained buried within the ocean's darkness, never to be spoken of again, as though the entire evening never happened.

CHAPTER 23

The following weeks adopted the same uneventful pace as before. Charlie called me once a week to see how I was getting on. We mostly talked about trivial matters, like conversations designed to merely pass the time. Quite honestly, I believe that he was worried about me, about my mental health, but he didn't want to come out and say it. Perhaps, he was concerned that guilt would overtake me and lead me to confess. We eventually and briefly discussed that night, but never spoke of it again. We both hoped that the haunting images and thoughts would someday leave us, but we knew better.

With the passing months, I had lost interest in the activities that I had once loved and enjoyed for the better part of my life, and the friendship that Charlie and I shared, most all of my friendships, for that matter, began dissolving. Everything was changing in my life, not overnight, but gradually, as though there was an unseen purpose behind it, some unknown driving force propelling me out of the old and into the new. There were days and nights that felt as if I had no direction, no purpose or place to go. I would find myself in dive bars, record shops, old bookstores, hell, even the Goodwill a few times, but my favorite was the shabby, movie theater that played the same two movies for two months straight. I'd go just about anywhere to avoid my old haunts. It wasn't long after the movie theater closed that I bought a used Ford Escort for $500 dollars. The only two things that thing had going for it was its engine and locking doors; beside that, the thing was a shit-box on wheels, but it was cheap, so I bought it. I was soon driving alone through the city streets in the winter rain, driving and getting lost, but always parking on overlooks, smoking cigarettes and listening to old songs on the radio— it was one of the loneliest times of my life.

I often thought of Delilah and of the possible reasons our paths crossed that night. There were countless nights spent staring at the ceiling waiting for the answer to enter my mind, but it never did, not truly, not without some sort of uncertainty attached to it. There were some nights were she couldn't have been any farther from my thoughts. Those were the good nights.

And without mincing words, there were nights she would return and crawl into my cold bed with me. She'd run freely in my dreams, talking and laughing and leaving her mark upon me, as though her presence was red lipstick being dragged along white walls of an endless hallway.

To be honest, the first six times she visited were the most terrifying. She had a penchant for waking me when she left, and it was always at 3:56 in the morning. She still continues to visit me in my sleep, but not as often. Now, I see her in the faces of other women. It occurs unexpectedly and feels, at least for a moment, that I've met these women before, but I know that it is merely my imagination playing another trick on me. I expect that I will never escape her reach for as long as I live.

EPILOGUE

Years have passed since that horrific night with Charlie, more years than I care to share. My parents have long sold their house, and most of my old friends have gotten married and moved away to far away cities where they can afford to buy houses and start families. People have carved out their paths, and it was rather appropriate. Hell, man, even Crumbs and Charlie found girlfriends and full-time work with benefits, and Ray, well, he graduated from a vocational school, and he has the certificate to prove it, as he so often says after a six pack of beer. He pays his union dues and works in construction and, as I suspected years ago, Ray never left the old neighborhood. He says, "Well, shit, man, someone had stay behind and watch over things, and it might as well be me. I ain't got a problem with it, never have." And, he was right.

Ray called my house late one evening, and intuition told me that something was terribly wrong. I was living in New York at that time of the call, but it still seems as if it was yesterday, because I'll never forget the seriousness in Ray's voice when he told me that Charlie had been killed in a car accident. I couldn't believe it— and I still don't want to believe it, but it's true, and there's not a damn thing I can do to change it. Occasionally, I weep at the thought and wonder if I'll ever stop. I remember the words Charlie so casually said to me during that last, long-distance phone call. He said, "Happiness is where we find it, Jacky, even if it's in a place no one else can see or understand. It's our own happiness that we must find, brother, no matter where it lies or what we must do to get there— we must get there."

I have never told anyone this secret or shared Charlie's final words, well, not until now. So, if you're asking, "Why now, Jack? What difference will it make?" To be honest, I'm not sure that it will make any difference at all or if you will even understand my reasoning, but I suppose, if had to offer an answer, my answer would be quite simple— I'm just trying to get there.

ABOUT THE AUTHOR

Ernest Langston is the author of the novel, *Born From Ashes*, and several screenplays. He resides in San Francisco, CA. For information, visit www.ernestlangston.com.

Printed in Great Britain
by Amazon

51113976R00144